Mist B Haven

Martha Steinhagen

Renuisance Press

LANSING, MICHIGAN

Renuisance Press
113 Allen Street
Lansing, Michigan 48912

Book Layout © 2014 BookDesignTemplates.com
Cover art and design Andrés García-Price
Author photo Yvonne Jardine Hubmayr

Mist B Haven/Martha Steinhagen. -- 1st ed.
ISBN 978-0-9981237-0-7 Print
ISBN 978-0-9981237-1-4 ePUB
ISBN 978-0-9981237-2-1 Kindle edition

For Kay Cornell and Rosemary Potts
who saved me

Prologue

I remember the day I looked in the mirror, humming some Beatles song about 'places I remember' and noticed the lines around my eyes and mouth. It's as if they arrived overnight and etched themselves a home on my face. Not that I really minded; it just came as a surprise. Kinda like 'Hey, look what just showed up on your face!' though they hadn't just shown up. It has taken years to create them, and I guess I saw them as they gradually arrived. But this day I looked up and there staring back at me was a familiar and yet changed face. And it shocked me to realize I am over seventy and lines are part of what comes with that. At least they are if you have lived any kind of life. Or maybe not just lived it, but experienced it, felt it. Survived the waves of troubles that crash over us, the swells of love or loss or grief. They leave a mark. Not just on the inside, but on the outside as well. And Lord knows, I have lived on the sea for most of my life, so waves and swells are a part of me.

Chapter One

I didn't mean to end up with a boat the day I left Dominic. I am not sure what I thought I would do. It was as if I stepped out for the proverbial pack of cigarettes and never turned back. Only my cigarette pack was called The *Mist B Haven* and it floated. I was sitting in a coffee shop, the old fashioned kind with booths and a waitress in a turquoise dress with stitching that said Biff's or some such on the apron. I had a cup of coffee and a clam roll in front of me. I had been looking out the window at the boats tied up in the marina, just smoking and drinking coffee and debating about whether I really wanted the clam roll, when a voice over my shoulder said "I am sick of her. I pour money and love in her and get back nothing but heart ache. I would give her away in a heartbeat but nobody will take her."

Funny way to talk about your wife or girlfriend, I thought, but then Dominic probably said much the same when he sat with his friends. I poured a little salt on the clam roll and turned and flagged the waitress for some cocktail sauce. Never could stomach that sweet weird tartar sauce they served with them. As I turned back I caught a glimpse of the two guys sitting behind me, a couple of old guys in suits and ties with their hats on the table beside them.

The non-speaker saw my look and laughed, "Not a woman, girlie. He's talking about his boat. And he doesn't really mean it, he's been saying that since I've known him about one boat or another. Think he'd learn. Don't buy a damn boat!" He chuckled when he said it, like it was hopeless and OK all at the same time.

"Nope, this time I really mean it, Ned. I am done with the boating life."

"Well," I said, picking up the clam roll, "I might like to give it a try."

And that is how I ended up standing in the head looking at my face in the mirror. Oh, it wasn't quite that simple.

Ned laughed, "Uh oh, Stan, girlie here is calling your bluff."

"What do you know about boats, kid?" the guy called Stan asked.

I liked that better than girlie, but not by much; felt like the old man was laughing at me. "I know they float and apparently they break your heart."

"How much money you got?"

"You said you were willing to give it away but nobody wanted it. Well, I do. I don't have any money."

"Everybody has *some* money, kid. How much you got in that purse there?"

"Twelve dollars and forty-seven cents, but I gotta pay for the coffee and the clam roll."

"Well, that ought to be enough to pay the dock fees for a month. You sure you want to own a boat?"

"Never really thought about it. How big is it?"

"Forty-eight foot."

"Hmmm." I was trying to buy time while I figured out how big that was.

"Ten booths," Ned offered. "It's yours plus ours and about eight more."

"Oh, my god, I could live on it!" I blurted out before I could stop myself.

"Oh girlie, you and several of your friends could live on it." he snorted. "What, don't you have a place to stay? Not that it's any of my bee's wax."

I liked him for saying that, bee's wax. I kept quiet, not wanting to answer, not really knowing the answer. I could go home to the apartment I shared with Dominic. I hadn't told him I was leaving. He was probably wondering where I was by now. But I realized sitting there that I didn't want to go back to that apartment, to that man. I wanted a new start and this seemed like maybe it could be that. No one would think to look for me at the marina, and maybe I could take the boat somewhere else eventually.

Stan sat quiet, watching me. "Pay yer bill and be sure to leave a nice tip for Lou Anne. I'll show you your new heartbreak."

The three of us walked out into the warm late afternoon sun and ambled down a series of wooden docks. Boats were tied up all along the way. "There she is," Stan stopped and gestured at the boat in front of us. It sat low in the water. "God damn bilge isn't working again," he muttered under his breath as he stepped over the rail and onto the deck of the boat. "Follow me. You might as well learn how to fix a bilge pump and bail a boat. Especially if you are going to take over this one."

Ned lit a cigarette and sat down in a sagging, broken down deck chair. "Jesus, Stan, when's the last time you were here? This thing looks like a garbage scow!"

"Shut up, Ned. I've been gone a while. You know that. Plus, I've been busy. Billy called to tell me I owed dock fees and that if I waited much longer I would have a permanent place on the bottom. Asshole. 'Scuse my language miss."

I had never been on a boat before. Hadn't seen the ocean till a year ago. But even I could tell this one needed a lot of work. The paint was peeling everywhere, the wood on the deck was cracked and dry, the railings were a tarnish color that I thought might be permanent. When Stan opened the cabin, the smell that oozed out was a mold, mildew, rotten food, and briny water combo. I wanted to light up to cover the smell, but Stan was moving deeper into the boat, motioning me to follow.

"God, Stan!" Ned was waving his hand in front of his scrunched up face. "What the hell is down there?"

"It's a boat goddammit. They smell rotten all the time."

I hoped that wasn't true because I was having trouble not gagging.

"Come on, kid, just gut it out. You'll get used to the smell in a minute." He led the way down a steep staircase into a V-shaped hallway that ended in a room with shallow bunks along both walls. "Hold up while I open the hatch." And with that he lifted the floor in front of me and shone a flash light into the darkness. "Shit." Water hovered about a foot from the top. "Shit. OK, come on, and bring that bucket with you."

Stan moved back down the hall and pulled up another section of floor at the base of the staircase. I could see another ladder. He disappeared down it. "Come on, kid, no dawdling!" The smell coming out of this hole added diesel fumes to the miasma of smells already swirling around me. I felt light-headed and reached out to steady myself on the wall.

My hand came away damp, sticky. The apartment was beginning to seem better and better.

"Come on. Come on! Bring the bucket and get down here."

I wasn't sure how to get down the ladder with any sense of dignity, so I gave up and hiked my skirt up over my knees, swung out over the trap door and clambered down the ladder. I stepped off into three inches of water and felt it immediately begin to soak my shoes. It was very close quarters, my head almost touched the ceiling. A small aisle ran down the middle with a big engine on either side. Stan was hunched over a smaller machine. His shoes and socks were perched on the engine and his pants were rolled nearly to his knees. "Here, give me the bucket." He grabbed it out of my hand, flipped it over and sat down on it. "This here is the bilge pump. There are a couple of them but this is the main one and it ain't working. That's why there is so much water in the hold and why we are sitting so low in the water."

"Are we sinking?"

"Nah. Well, maybe. If I can't get this thing running again and if you can't bail fast enough. But I think she'll be all right. Hasn't sunk yet!"

He pulled a wrench off a ledge over the pump and began to open it up. "Ah, see here, this wire is loose and isn't making a connection. Should be able to strip it out and reconnect it and Bob's your uncle."

"Huh?"

"You know, everything will be Jake. A-OK, Okey-dokey."

"Oh."

And it was. Stan fixed the wire and the pump started pumping and the water level dropped and the boat floated higher in the water and we didn't sink.

Chapter Two

"Okay, she's no prize I admit." Stan leaned over the rail and flipped his cigarette overboard. He had rolled his pants back down and put his shoes on. I perched on the corner of a small wooden shelf along the back of the boat, water leaking out of mine. Ned still sat in the sagging chair. "I let her go a bit. But she has good bones. She just needs a little TLC and a lot of elbow grease to get her shipshape again. Once you open up the salon doors and portholes, the smell will lessen and it will seem a bit nicer. Here, I'll show you around."

And he did. He referred to everything by its nautical name, the main deck and the salon, which looked like a combination living room and dining room. The galley, which was just another way of saying kitchen. The upper deck, which had the wheelhouse where the instruments and the actual wheel to steer the boat were. The foredeck, which was out in front of the wheelhouse and was totally empty. But I could imagine deck chairs and loungers scattered about. There was a very small cabin behind the wheelhouse with a narrow bed and desk for the captain, apparently.

Down below, there were two cabins. One larger one with a big bed and built in drawers and bookshelves. And the one we had been in with the bunk beds. Stan called it a V-berth, because of the way it followed the line of the hull and flared out from the floor like a V. There were two heads, bathrooms, both tiny but adequate. One in the master cabin and one on the main deck. They both were a kind of combo toilet with shower above. I guess the whole room got wet if you showered!

"So what do you think, girlie?" Ned asked as we returned from the tour. My eyes must have looked like saucers. He laughed. "Think you want to be a seafaring gal?"

I nodded, afraid my voice would give away just how much I wanted to stay right there on the *Mist B Haven* and never leave.

"Well, if you think you can handle it, she's all yours." Stan chimed in. "I think you will appreciate her and I really am done with the boating life."

Ned rolled his eyes. "That will be the day!" he scoffed in a friendly way.

"No really, Ned. I have no more use for this thing and I would rather she be cared for than sink here at the dock because I don't come fix the bilge someday. You said yourself she stinks and looks like a garbage scow. A boat like this doesn't deserve that. She needs someone to love her and I think the kid here might fit the bill."

I nodded again, trying to look confident.

"I will stop by in a few days and sign her over to you. In the meantime, I paid the dock fee for a month. After that it's on you. There is a Captain's Log in the wheelhouse that will help you get acquainted with the boat and her systems. A copy of *Chapman's Seamanship* is on the shelf with it. Should cover just about anything you need to know. Otherwise you might ask Billy, the dock master, or see if one of the other boaties can help you. Good luck to you, kid."

He swung his leg over the rail and stepped up onto the dock. "Come on, Ned. Leave the girl to explore."

They both tipped their hats and walked off down the pier, leaving me alone on the deck of a boat I knew nothing about but her name.

Chapter Three

My first night on board was hardly living at the Ritz. None of the beds had linens on them and the damp seemed to invade the entire boat. I huddled under a thin, mildewy blanket I found stuffed in a corner of the main cabin. But cold and uncomfortable as I was, I was also excited at the prospect of owning a boat. This boat. This big, old, broken-down boat.

The sun woke me up, that and some guy hollering "hallooo the boat". I had no idea what that meant but the voice was loud and nearby. I climbed up to the main deck and peeked out the salon door to see who was shouting.

"Ah, so there is someone on board! Good morning. I'm Alf. I live a couple slips down on the Swede Sea. You look like you could use some coffee. Come on over when you're ready. Dark green hull, white cabin." And that was my introduction to boatie life. I tried using the head but couldn't get the toilet to flush. Where is the handle? Ran my fingers through my hair. I could get no water from the tap to wash my face. Gave it all up, straightened my skirt and set off to find Alf's boat.

I found his boat and him four slips down from mine. He was sitting on the main deck having the most delicious smelling coffee. "Come on board, I have a cup right here with your name on it. You good with regular coffee or should I go find the instant Sanka?"

"Regular is good with me." I sank into the most comfortable looking chair and wrapped my hands around the heavy coffee mug, grateful for the warmth.

"Gets a bit nippy at night out on the water. You might want to wear a sweater when you come visit next time. We all live outside mostly."

"Is that because everyone's boat smells as bad as mine?"

"No," he laughed. "It's because boaties like to be outside looking at the water, not all cooped up inside looking at paneling or whatever. Your boat smells bad?"

"Like the worst root cellar you have ever been in crossed with the smell of truck exhaust."

"Well, that isn't normal. Here come on inside and I will show you."

Alf crossed the deck and opened the cabin door. I hung back expecting the same sickening smell the *Mist B Haven* carried. I stepped cautiously over the door jam and waited to be smothered. Nothing, just coffee and a hint of lemon. "Wow. It's like a lemon orchard in here."

"That's the lemon oil I use on the teak. Keeps it shiny and happy."

"What's teak?"

"That would be all the wood you see in here. This boat has a lot of it. Some don't. You want the tour?"

I nodded, sipping the hot coffee.

"Won't take but a minute. This is the main deck, small salon, tiny galley, nice back deck for sitting on, but you already saw that. Up the ladder is the helm station; below this deck is my cabin and the engine room. Got a little head in the cabin. And there you have it. Not much room to walk around, and you see why I like to sit outside. The view is way better and I like open space." He opened the door of the salon and stepped back outside. I liked his boat. It was small but very neat and tidy. Shipshape began to have a real meaning to me. Everything seemed to have a place. Shelves were tucked into corners and out of the way spaces. Nothing wasted. It felt cozy. And for a moment I wished for a smaller boat. Which made me laugh out loud since up until twelve hours ago I had no boat, or any plan to have one!

Alf looked over his shoulder at me and smiled. "So Stan finally found someone to buy that old tub of his."

That caught me off guard. Should I tell him I had paid nothing? Would he think I was a freeloader or a con artist tricking Stan out of his boat? Had he heard Stan gave it to me and he was checking it out? Did he know I had nowhere else to go? Suddenly I wanted off this boat and away from this nice man with his warm coffee and prying questions.

"Whoa, no offense meant. Everyone calls their boat a tub at some point! Didn't mean to insult you or your boat. Here warm up your coffee and set a spell."

Fortunately for me he had mistaken my panic at answering his question for offense. A bit more delay and the question might be forgotten. I poured a bit more coffee from the thermos he handed me. "OK. No worries. I am a bit new to the boating world. I guess I have a lot to learn! Tub seems like a good place to start."

"Yeah, I kind of figured you for a newbie."

"What gave me away?"

"Well, most folks don't usually wear business clothes on boats."

I looked down at the once crisp white blouse and gabardine skirt, now both wrinkled and sad looking. My nylons had a run in them and my shoes were still a soggy mess from standing in the bilge water. "So what do boat people wear if not business clothes?"

"Well, most boaties are men so they wear khakis or cutoff jeans or clamdiggers for fancy occasions, and tee shirts. Flip flops or topsiders for shoes, though mostly we all go barefoot. A good pair of RayBans and a cap of some kind. Need to keep the sun off your nose. Or it will end up looking like mine...hamburger."

"Hmmm." I thought about the $9.75 I still had in my purse and my closet full of dresses and skirts at the apartment. Neither seemed likely to provide me with clothes that would fit the bill. "Well perhaps I will add a more formal look to the boating world." How I was going to wash and iron my blouse when I couldn't get water to wash my hands or flush the toilet was going to present a problem. That and I didn't have a second set of clothes to wear while I washed these.

Perhaps Alf had begun to get a sense of my situation, or maybe he already knew I was here with nowhere else to go and very little money. Maybe Ned or Stan asked him to look after me. I don't know and he never told me. But he was about to help me for the first of many times over the years.

"Well, you look to be the size of my first and last mate. Little bastard ran off with some of my money soon as we docked here last spring. Don't reckon he will be back for his stuff. Pardon my language, miss. Been a sailor too long not to swear every now and then. No disrespect meant."

"None taken. I think if I am going to hang around with sailors, I will get used to it."

He snorted in a friendly way. "Sit tight. I'll see if I can find the stuff."

When he returned, he had an arm load of clothes and a couple thick wool blankets. "This ought to set you up to start with. I know that gal Stan had around here for a while made off with most everything that wasn't bolted down, so I thought you might need a blanket or two. These are extras I carry in case I fish someone out of the drink. But I think you need them more, and I am not planning on going out any time soon. Feel free to keep them as long as you need."

"I don't know what to say, Alf. I haven't really had time or daylight to figure out what is on the boat and what I need. This will certainly help. Next up is some lemon oil so my boat smells as good as yours!"

"Sounds like you need bleach more than lemon oil. You need to scrub everything down with bleach to get rid of the mold and mildew. That will help the smell right off the bat."

"Great idea. If I only knew how to get water, I would be all set!"

"You ever been on a boat before?"

"Nope, not till last night."

"Come on, I'll take a look at what you got and see if we can't figure out how to hook you up with water."

And that is how Alf and I started to become friends. He gave me clothes and blankets and my first lesson in boating life. When you don't know something, ask another boater. They may not know but they will happily poke around until they figure it out or break something.

Chapter Four

Fortunately, Alf didn't break anything and he knew how to connect the boat to the dock water and electricity so I could have lights as well.

"Once you get yourself squared away you can start to figure out how to charge your own batteries and run off them so you don't run up a big dock bill. Same with water. I have a catch system to collect rain water to supplement the dock water. You might have a desalinization system on board. But for now you are all set."

"This is great, Alf. Thanks for showing me how to do this. Now I can start the clean up!"

"Might want to start with yourself, kiddo," he laughed as he stepped back on to the dock and turned towards his boat. "See you around, swabby."

I wasn't sure that was a good thing to be called but he was right. I did need to get out of the clothes I had been wearing for the past day and a half. A shower sounded good, too, now that I had access to water. If only I had asked him to show me how to flush the toilet! I just couldn't bring myself to ask. Luckily the shower in the master stateroom was very much like a normal land shower. I found an old bar of soap and used a rusted knife I found in the galley to scrape off the old goo and provide a fairly fresh bar. It felt good to stand under the spray, though Alf had warned me that water conservation was a must as a boater. The lukewarm water certainly encouraged brevity.

I rummaged through the clothes and found a pair of khakis that fit surprisingly well (one good thing about a boyish figure, I guess) and a white tee shirt, both of which smelled freshly laundered and felt soft against my skin. I wasn't used to wearing pants, for women in the late fifties and early sixties, skirts or dresses were standard attire. But the pants felt comfortable and practical, given how much going up and down ladders I was doing.

The whole day stretched out in front of me and I needed to get organized, devise a plan so I didn't get overwhelmed and just sit and stare, doing nothing. Cleaning did seem to be the first order of business. I wasn't sure where to start since everything needed attention. I decided on the master stateroom, or what I was beginning to think of as my cabin. If I had a relatively clean and tidy place to curl up in, I felt like I could tolerate chaos everywhere else.

First up was figuring out the toilet. Stan had said there was a Captain's Log in the wheelhouse and that seemed like the best place to start, unless I wanted to ask Alf or some other stranger, which so far I wasn't willing to do. I found the log which turned out to be a notebook of entries about where the *Mist B Haven* had been, what the weather was like, sea conditions, passengers on board, but nothing about how to flush the toilet! Next up Chapman's. This turned out to be a volume about the size of a cinder block. Well, OK, maybe not that big, more like a very comprehensive dictionary. Which is partly what it was. It seemed to have a section on just about anything having to do with a boat. How to sail, what each sail was called and when they were best used. Thank goodness, I didn't have to learn all that! Engines are complicated but once they start, so do you. Not like the wind and figuring out how to go straight when the wind is blowing from the side. Whew. According to Chapman's all I had to do was steer towards where I wanted to go. If I ever got that far.

I was happy to find that Chapman's does indeed have a whole section on marine heads and there was a drawing that looked a lot like mine. I took the book below and set it up so I could read while I went step by step through the process. Open this valve at the base of the head, pull the pump handle up and pump until satisfied. Lock down pump, close lower valve. Success! It even suggested that a bit of Pinesol poured in after the flush would help keep the head smelling good, or at least not nasty. I put Pinesol on my list of supplies to get along with lemon oil, bleach and food.

With flushing figured out, I decided to inventory what I had in the way of supplies on board so I would know what I needed and what I already had. I started at the lowest point of the boat and would work my way up. That meant starting in the engine room. The bilge pump was still running, so that was a good sign. There were various tools scattered about. I collected them and arranged them on a shelf above one of the engines. It had a tall lip so nothing would roll out, and a net to pull across to secure everything. Wrenches, pliers, a hammer, various screw drivers and a number of things I was pretty sure were tools but I wasn't sure what they did or their names. Didn't really matter, up on the shelf they went. Cans of oil and grease went on the opposite wall; same set up, pull a net across to secure everything. I was tempted to start cleaning, but so far I had no cleaning supplies. I reminded myself this was just an inventory tour.

I checked the compartment that had been nearly full of water yesterday. It was empty but for a couple of inches of water on the floor. This seemed a vast improvement over nearly flooded. I closed it up and went on. The V-berth was next. Two sets of bunk beds with moldy, damp, stained mattresses. Before I could stop myself, I had grabbed one and was dragging it out and up onto the back deck. Once I had a stack of four I decided that this was the trash heap and I would off load it all once I was done. The V-berth also had a small closet that had a couple old yellow mackinaws with rain pants to match. I hung these on the upper rail to get some sun on the damp fabric in hopes they would eventually air out. I also found a small bookshelf with a collection of paperbacks with racy covers. I decided to air them out and then return them to the shelf. Never know how bored I might get. The walls and bunks would eventually need to be scrubbed down with bleach to kill the mold and mildew and whatever else was growing there. I didn't really want to think about it too long.

On to the master stateroom. This cabin looked like it had been used more recently and by a person with a higher degree of cleanliness. The mattress was newer and cleaner though it was still damp and a little smelly. I dragged it up top too but decided I needed to sleep on something and it was the last soft thing around, so it didn't go on the trash pile. I found a spot with a good bit of sun and laid it there, hoping for magic. The drawers and closet were empty. Alf was right. Someone had taken pretty much everything. But with a good cleaning, I felt like this would be a cozy place to curl up at night. I noticed the portholes along one wall. They were coated with grime but once clean would bring in a fair amount of light.

The galley was next. It had a two burner gas stove and a small ice box, literally, an ice box. Put in a block of ice and keep stuff sort of cool. Might work. There was a sink and a rack of shelves which obviously used to hold pots and pans and dishware. All gone now, of course. I added pan, plate, cup, bowl, sharp knife and fork to my list of supplies. I would also need to figure out gas for the stove. The portholes here were bigger (higher above the water line Alf explained to me later) but they were just as dirty. The salon was mostly built-in benches with cushions around the perimeter of the room, a banquette with a good size table and a wall of shelves also empty, but I could see them filled with books. I dragged the cushions out for the sun treatment and realized when I moved them the benches were actually storage compartments. I am not sure what went in them, nothing there now, but it seemed like a clever use of the space. I figured eventually I would find a use for them.

The wheelhouse was fairly bare. The big wheel to steer with, a stool bolted to the floor in front of it, and a large built-in table opposite it was the extent of that area. A bench ran under the table along the back wall. I pulled the cushion out onto the upper deck so it could air out as well. The small room behind the wheelhouse held a built-in bed, a desk, and a dresser of sorts. The mattress joined the cushions in the sun on deck. I pulled open the dresser drawers expecting them to be empty like everything else. But assumptions can sometimes get you killed.

Chapter Five

There wasn't any big explosion, but there might as well have been. The drawer was stuffed with money. Not fives or tens. Nope these bills had Ben Franklin and U.S. Grant on them. I slammed the drawer closed and looked around. No one here to see this, but I'm telling you, you find a drawer full of money and you'd look around, too! I opened the next drawer and it looked about as stuffed as the first one. Three drawers, all of them full of money. And none of it was mine. But whose was it? Not the woman who had taken everything else. Clearly she never got around to these drawers. Stan's? Did he give me the boat and forget he had a ton of dough stashed aboard? Seemed unlikely. But whose then? Maybe the person whose cabin I was standing in...the captain. But why would he leave all this money on an empty, untended boat? No one had been here in a while. The dust on the top of the dresser was undisturbed and fairly deep. It wasn't like he was keeping tabs on it. Where did it all come from and how could Stan not know about it? I opened the small closet above the dresser, afraid that there would be some other surprise waiting. Empty. No more money, thank goodness.

My supply list was getting longer; linens, pillow, a second bra and underwear so I could wash one and wear one. A warm coat, a sweater, bleach, scrub brushes and sponges, maybe a second bucket. Long list and nine dollars and change in my purse. I opened the top drawer and chose a U.S. Grant. Make that two, and closed the drawer. I would pay whomever back once I got a job, but right now this was my loan office.

It felt odd to walk off the boat knowing all that cash was up top. But I decided to try and forget it was there and just go about my business. It was lunch time and I stopped into the coffee shop for a sandwich and a coffee. I was hoping to see Stan or Ned, but even though the place was crowded I didn't see them. I sat down at the counter. The waitress from yesterday set a coffee mug in front of me and ask what I wanted. Hot dog and fries seemed like a good change of pace.

"It's Lou Anne, right?"

She nodded as she set the plate in front of me. "Have you seen Stan or Ned, the two guys that were here yesterday?"

"Nope."

"Do they eat here often?"

"I never seen them before yesterday."

"But they knew your name."

"Honey, anyone who can read knows my name." She pointed to a black plastic name tag with Lou Anne in big white block letters.

"Oh, right." I ate my hot dog, paid the bill, left a nice tip and headed out. I had no idea where to begin to find the kind of stores that would have the items on my list. I headed back to Alf's boat to see if he could steer me in the right direction.

"Heck, I'll go with you. I love to shop."

"No man likes to shop."

"Well, I do. Gives me something to do other than work on the boat or stare out at the water. You wait, couple months and you'll be looking forward to shopping! Show me your list so I know which way to head."

I handed over the crumpled paper.

"Okay, the bra and panties I might not be that helpful with but everything else we can get at the Piggly Wiggly and the marine supply store. Follow me."

Alf had a rolling walk, like he was still on the boat. It looked kind of funny with his bow legs sticking out of his cut off jeans. His flip flops made a cheery sound as they flapped against the pavement. I realized I must look odd too, pants and a tee shirt and a pair of water stained heels. "Can we get flip flops and shoes first? I look ridiculous in these."

"Yep, that's where we are headed."

It was a good thing Alf came along. By the time we were finished we were both loaded down with packages. "I should have brought my wagon."

"You have a car?"

"No, I have a little red wagon that I take with me when I shop to carry all my stuff home in. I just forgot to bring it. Didn't think you would have such a long list! Silly of me, you are starting out. It always takes a lot to start."

I stepped over the rail of the *Mist B Haven* and dropped my packages on the deck. I knew I should invite Alf in, but the state and smell of the boat wasn't really guest friendly.

"Here take these off my hands" He shoved the packages at me. "I got to go check my bilge pump. Stop over later for a beer and sunset if you like." And off he rolled down the dock.

Chapter Six

Cleaning has never been a favorite job of mine, but the thought of sleeping in the dust and grime was incentive enough to get started. I headed down to "my" cabin with a bucket of water and bleach and started scrubbing at the door. I opened each porthole once I had cleaned the inside and the breeze off the water smelled fresh and salty. I dragged the mattress in from the deck and made the bed with new pads and sheets and the blankets Alf had given me. I put my hand-me-down clothes away in the now clean dresser and put my shoes on the floor of the closet. The room smelled clean and looked bright and inviting. It made me happy to look around.

The salon and galley were next and, by the time the sun was setting, the main living areas were livable.

"Halloo the boat," called a familiar voice. "Permission to come aboard? I have refreshments!"

I was hot and dirty and one of the sweating beers in Alf's hand would sure taste good. "Come aboard, come aboard!"

"I figured if you weren't coming to me for the sunset, I would have to come to you."

"I lost track of time, sorry."

"No problem, I just thought someone should be here with you to toast your first full day on the water. Here's to calm seas and starry nights. Cheers."

"Cheers, Alf. And thanks."

We sat quietly leaning against the rail (deck chairs go on the next list, I thought) and watched the sun go down.

"Hey, Alf, how about a tour?"

"Thought you'd never ask!"

And with that I opened the salon door and welcomed my first visitor to the Mist B Haven.

Chapter Seven

I spent most of the next week slowly cleaning and organizing the boat. I scrubbed and oiled and polished. Once I got the inside looking good, I started on the outside. I scrubbed and oiled and polished and then all that was left was scraping and painting the hull and the exterior of the boat. Alf gave me some tips and though it was slow going, the boat began to look like someone cared about it again. It began to have a happy feeling about it. Alf would bring beers and sit on the deck rail and comment on my progress. It really helped to have someone else notice the changes.

"So, do you think you will ever go anywhere on this boat?" he asked one evening.

"You know, sometimes I forget that this is a boat. Well, not really forget, but it doesn't seem real that I could go somewhere."

"Hell, that's what a boat is for! I'm fixing to be motoring off to warmer climes here pretty soon."

The idea of sitting in the marina without Alf for company was a new thought to me. It hadn't occurred to me that he wasn't a permanent resident of the marina.

"You should think about moving south, too. See the world. Boats weren't meant to sit in harbor for very long. Have you ever even cranked up the engines on her?"

And then it hit me. I was thinking of this boat not as a mobile home, but as a stationary apartment that I was fixing up, but would eventually leave, like I had everywhere else I had ever lived. The boat could allow me to leave someplace without ever leaving my home. This could be my home forever. But this location didn't have to be. I suddenly felt free in a secure way that I never had before. I could wander and yet always have my home with me!

"I haven't. In fact, I have no idea how to start them or how to make the boat move. But I think that is where I am going to turn my attention. Because you are right, I need to move on."

Chapter Eight

Chapman's was becoming my bedtime reading. It had chapters on weather and docking a boat with one or two engines and how to steer and what different lights mean, and knot tying. It was a cross between a dictionary, an encyclopedia, a *Bible* and the *Boy Scout Handbook*. Very handy to have. But a real live person was even better. I would read at night and ask Alf questions over coffee or beers.

"You know there is a Coast Guard captain's license class starting Monday. Why don't you sign up? It would teach you a lot of the theory of boating, and how to read a chart, and plotting, and rules of the road, and all of the book stuff you need to know to motor around safely. You take the class and I will give you driving lessons. How to get the boat in and out of a slip and how to steer in open, rough water. Then you would be ready to go whenever you wanted."

"Are you a Coast Guard Captain?"

"Nope, but I'm not a girl either."

"What's that supposed to mean?"

"Just that boaties tend to be men. Sometimes you see women in the marina but they are usually with some guy who is running the boat. Folks will always assume that you don't know what you are doing and they will give you a hard time. But if you have a license it will shut them up, because most of them are like me, unlicensed skippers. You aren't required to have a license unless you are being a captain for money or you carry a certain number of passengers."

"But you think if I have a license, people, men, won't give me a hard time?"

"Oh, they still will. It just might shut them up sooner."

So I raided the cash drawer again and signed up for the course. Two weeks later I had a certificate to hang on the wall that said I was a Coast Guard licensed captain. Now if only I felt like one.

Alf and I had been working on the engines, they were badly in need of attention. Oil change, air filter change, clean out the fuel filter and the injectors, replace a cracked Raycor bowl, charge the batteries, clean the contacts, check the props and the drive shafts. It seemed to go on and on. The bad news was I had two engines to repair and then maintain. The good news was I had two engines. Alf worked on one while I did exactly what he was doing on the other. Real hands-on experience. And when we cranked them over and mine started just a shade sooner than his, a flush of pride shot through me.

With working engines and a nice piece of paper on the wall that said I was a captain, I set out to learn how to be one. Alf showed me how to cast off the lines that held the *Mist B Haven* to the dock. He had me stand next to him while he pulled the boat out of the slip, explaining each thing he was doing. When to put which engine in gear and how much throttle to give it. And suddenly we were out past the breakwater in open ocean, just Alf and me and the boat and an endless horizon. Unbelievable for a person who had never seen the ocean till a year ago. It was heaven.

"Oh, Alf," I sighed.

"I know, pretty amazing, isn't it? And this is always here...and if you have a boat, it is always available."

"I have a boat."

"Yes, you do."

Alf showed me how to steer into the sea and with following seas which I learned meant taking the waves on my bow (front) or taking waves on my stern (back). I learned how to travel at an angle to the wave to have it affect the boat less. We practiced what happened with only one engine. The boat steered to the right or left depending on which engine was engaged.

"This comes in handy when you are docking or trying to get out of a slip," he explained. "You can get the boat to pull in using the engines. Twin props are great for that. I'm jealous. I just have the one engine. Makes the mechanics simpler and running costs cheaper, but boy, having two engines sure can be convenient. And a lot easier when one dies."

"God, Alf. What do you do when your engine conks out? That can happen, right?"

"Yep, and I run down below as fast as I can and try to fix it as quick as I can. Otherwise I just float around at the mercy of the sea. Not very much fun, I got to tell you."

"You're right. I am glad I have two. Especially since I am not sure I could fix it."

"Well, you learn fast out here, and that's why you need to practice as much as you can. Not just driving but taking things apart and understanding how they work. 'Cuz it is going to be just you someday...you and the big bad ocean and you best have an idea about how to help yourself. Or be a really good swimmer."

The magnitude of what I was doing was continuing to sink in. Alf was right. I needed to know way more than I did since it was going to be just me. Something I was beginning to like...being just me, but also something that could have major consequences. Life-altering consequences or life-ending ones.

I really was going to be responsible for myself. Me, no one else. It was both exhilarating and terrifying at the same time.

"Okay. Point her in towards the channel and I'll show you how to dock this tub." That got a laugh out of both of us.

Chapter Nine

"Starboard forward, port reverse. Jesus, Girl, did you forget everything I taught you?"

We had been practicing every day for almost a week and I was still having trouble docking. "Can't you just say left and right?" I snarled back.

"Well I could, but only a land lubber would say that on a boat."

"So fine, I'm a land lubber! Why can't we just say left and right!"

"Because it isn't left and right. It is this side of the boat and that side of the boat no matter which way you are standing. See if I turn and face the stern and you say left, well, that is *that* direction to me." He pointed one way. "And that direction to you," he pointed the opposite direction. "So which is it? Left or right? But if you say port it is always the left side of the boat when facing forward. So if I turn around and face the stern and you say port, it's the left side of the boat when facing forward, no matter which way I am facing. Understand? It is like in a car. There is the passenger's side and the driver's side. I say turn towards the driver's side, well, no matter what way you are facing you know which side that is. It is the same on a boat, but the driver stands in the middle, so we say port and starboard to note a specific side of the boat. This side is always port. Even if you were hanging upside down, the left side of the boat when facing forward is port. Period."

"Okay. I just have trouble remembering which is which."

"Port is short like left and starboard is longer like right. Does that help?"

"Yes a little. It's just going to take me some time to get it straight in my mind and not always have to think port, left if facing forward."

"Think of it like learning a foreign language. Eventually you will stop translating in your head and you will be dreaming in Spanish, or nautical in this case."

It took several more weeks of practice before I felt secure in my general abilities running the boat. And then one day I headed down the dock with a cup of coffee for Alf and the *Swede Sea* slip was empty. There was an envelope stuck to one of the dock posts. "Girl" it said on the front. And I knew it was for me and that Alf was gone.

Chapter Ten

I had to go this way. Goodbyes have never been that successful for me. And I have a feeling we will cross paths again on the blue sea and I will be very happy to see you. You have turned yourself into a pretty fair little mariner. You have a good feel for your boat and for the seas and you are a quick study. That might not always work in your favor but in this area it has. I have taught you about all I can. Now it is up to you to venture out and learn what you don't know and then go find someone or something to teach you. It has been very special for me to help you. Making up for the ways I didn't teach my own daughter what she needed to know, I guess. I couldn't say any of this to you in person. Just not my way. But I want you to know how impressed I am with your determination and your spunk. And how proud I am to know you.

You know enough. You can go wherever you want. Go. Go see the world. I'll be looking for you. Untie your boat, untie yourself and motor out. You can. I believe it. I wouldn't have left otherwise.

I wish light winds and following seas for you. But always keep a life jacket nearby and your radio on channel one six.

I'll miss you, Girl.

Alf

I realized I had been reading through tears. I folded up Alf's letter and stuck it in the pocket of a pair of cutoffs he'd given me. He had given me everything, and I was too wrapped up in myself to notice or say a proper thank you. I should have noticed he was getting ready to leave he was coming back to his boat with his wagon stuffed with provisions. He told me he was headed for warmer climes. I just didn't believe he would leave so soon and without a proper goodbye. I slumped down on the deck of my boat and sobbed.

I was alone. Me and a forty-eight-foot boat.

Chapter Eleven

Eventually I cried myself out. I wiped my face with the hem of my tee shirt and stood up. Time to get moving. Get a plan and get moving. Quit feeling sorry for yourself, some internal voice declared. You are a big girl. Start acting like one. Enough of the sniveling. I went up to the wheelhouse and pulled out the charts Alf and I had been practicing on. I could go down the Intracoastal waterway all the way to Florida and then on anywhere in the Atlantic or the Caribbean from there. If I went out into the open seas it would be faster but the conditions would be much more variable and challenging. I didn't feel quite up to that, plus I could stop along the way to earn money and re-provision the boat if I chose the Intracoastal route. And from looking at the charts, it seemed if I got bored or wanted a challenge I could put out into open water all along the way.

One of the few things holding me back was the fact that Stan had never returned to sign the boat over to me. Lately I had begun to wonder if it really was his boat. I wasn't even sure how to confirm it, but I was beginning to think it was important to find out. I rinsed my face, pulled on a cleaner tee shirt and some long pants and headed up to the Coast Guard station. They might know how to research it. Was it like a car? Or a house? I wasn't sure.

The Coastie at the desk wasn't sure either, he sent me down the hall to the next guy. He actually did know. "Bring in the registration number and the hull number and I think I can help you. How big is the boat?"

"Forty-eight foot."

"Yep, that is probably a federal registration. So we should be able to help."

"Great. Where do I find these numbers?"

"Well, the registration number should be painted on the bow of the boat somewhere, and the hull number should be stamped or cast into the transom. Look in the engine room on the support beams, see if you see anything there."

Clearly he could see my puzzlement. Nautical folks love their nautical talk!

"Once you have the numbers we can research the Coast Guard Registry."

"Huh, and how long will that take?"

"Couple weeks I would guess."

"No way to speed that up? "

"Not unless the boat is registered locally with this branch office. Then we could find it pretty quickly."

"Okay, thanks." I wasn't sure if a salute was required so I just went back down the hall and out the door I came in.

The registration numbers were visible from halfway down the dock, now that I knew what I was looking for. The hull numbers were a bit harder but eventually I found them under a layer of grime on the support strut over the engines. I realized in the process that more cleaning was in order if I wanted a really shipshape boat. But first things first. I trooped back to the CG Station and handed the numbers to my new Coastie friend.

"Okay. I will start checking first thing tomorrow. Why don't you stop by tomorrow afternoon and I will at least know if it was registered here locally or if you have a longer wait ahead of you."

"Great. See you tomorrow afternoon."

"Oh and bring two bucks, that's the fee for a local search. National will cost you ten."

"Gotcha, thanks."

Now it was just a waiting game. I wasn't sure what I was going to do if Stan didn't own the boat. I had been living on it for almost two months and the elbow grease alone felt like a big investment on my part. I didn't want to discover someone else owned it and they could just show up and order me off. I had become quite fond of the *Mist B Haven*.

Rather than continue to worry, I decided a good engine room clean was in order. That ate up most of the rest of my day. With no Alf calling me topside for a beer and sunset, I almost missed it. But I managed to get to the upper deck just as the last of the orange ball disappeared into the water. Swallowed up for another day. The dark brought back all the fears and I could find nothing to do to calm them. I decided to get the Captain's Log and start reading it. If Stan wasn't the owner, maybe it would tell me who was. And there was still the drawers of money to account for. Admittedly the top drawer was a bit less crammed than when I climbed aboard the *Mist B Haven*. Running the engines required fuel and fuel cost money. Alf had never asked me where I got my money and I never told him. Of course I never asked him about his either. It seemed boaters were a friendly but private group. At least the ones I had met. Alf used to say every boatie he ever met was running away from something. Asking what just made people unhappy and what was the point of that?

I retrieved the thick log from the helm station and curled up on my berth. I decided to work backwards from the most recent entry to the first. I figured the information I needed would be recent not ancient history. I pulled the waterlogged book to me and opened it to the last page. Blank. Well, of course it was. This was a big book and it had room for much more to be written. So I paged back through the blank pages until I found an entry. It was dated three days ago. Alf. He had logged all our trips out of the marina.

October 15, 1960 1500 hours

Practiced quartering waves and engine failure drills. Deployed and retrieved the life raft. Checked all systems and emergency supplies. Flares up to date and stowed safely. Shot off one outdated flare. Checked life rings and jackets. All dry and properly stowed. All is set and in order. First mate is trained and ready to assume command of vessel.

Good sailing, Girl.

Captain Alf Lidstrom

And that brought the tears all over again. I put the logbook down turned out the light and cried myself to sleep for the first time since I was a little girl.

Chapter Twelve

I spent the next morning reading the rest of Alf's log entries. He had logged each time we left the marina, where we had gone, what we had done, when we left and when we returned. It was like a movie of us without the sound and picture. His descriptions were concise and vivid; I could see us clearly in my mind's eye. It was like reliving it. Almost like hearing Alf's voice inside my head. I missed him.

I stopped reading when I got to Alf's first entry. I would read the next person's entries when I got back from the Coast Guard station. I decided to treat myself to lunch, so I headed up to the diner.

"Hey, Lou Anne." I felt like I knew her. I came in a couple times a week so she at least was familiar with my face. She gave me a hurried smile, nodded at an open seat at the counter and kept on towards a booth in the back.

"What'll it be, honey?"

"Tuna salad sandwich, fries and coffee please."

"Gotcha. You want me to bring it here or to the booth where your friends are?"

"Alf's here?' I asked hopefully.

"No, your other friends, the two guys you always ask me about."

I turned in the direction of her nod and there was Ned happily waving me over.

"Hey, girlie, come join us!"

I took my coffee and slid into the booth on Ned's side. Stan moved their hats to the seat next to him and smiled. "So how goes the life of a mariner, kid?"

Fortunately, Lou Anne arrived with my sandwich, so I had a moment to think. "Well, it's been a lot to learn and the boat took a while to get clean and fixed up. She looks great now." I said proudly and then it occurred to me that maybe he was here to take it back. I worried if I said too much about how great she was he might decide she wasn't that much trouble and want her back. Maybe he would realize she was worth more money now, since I had been working on her and restoring her to a sea worthy vessel, and he wanted money from me. Oh man, money! Maybe he was here to get his money. Would he notice the $420 I had 'borrowed' from the drawers? I had records of what I had done with every dollar, but it still wasn't my money to use. How would I pay him back?

Ned sensed my sudden change in mood. "What's wrong? Sandwich taste bad?"

"No, it's fine."

"Don't worry." Stan interrupted, "We were just here to have a coffee before we came to find you and let you know I signed the boat over to you."

"Stan, are you sure you still want to do that?"

"Why? Are you sick of owning a boat already? Is it too much for you?"

"No, no, none of that. I love the boat, I love living on it and working on it. I just don't understand why you would give it to me?"

"Ah, you mean what's the catch?"

I nodded, not able to speak. I *so* didn't want there to be a catch, but it only seemed logical that there would be one. I waited.

"Well, I'll tell you. I have owned a boat since I was a young man, not all of them were like the *Mist B Haven*. Some were small little row boats practically, but I have always had a boat. And for the last fifteen years they have brought me very little pleasure. Oh, I like being out on the water. It's all the other stuff I don't like. Cleaning and polishing, hiring a crew, paying for someone else to sit on *my* boat and clean and polish. It's never ending with a boat. And the past five years I have kept the boat to impress my business associates and their wives and clients. I haven't really had that boat for me. It became a money drain and an energy drain. More of an energy drain than something fun. I got more and more sick of it. I just want to have a little Boston Whaler to run around the harbor in and see if I can't be happy out on the water again. But I am done with big boats. Nothing over fifteen feet for me ever again. I was busy shooting off my big mouth and you called my bluff, as Ned said, and I realized, I would be happy to be free of her."

"But she is worth a lot of money, or at least I think she is."

"Yep, she probably is and my soon to be ex-wife is really looking forward to taking it away from me because she thinks it will hurt me."

"So you are doing this to get back at your wife?

"Ex-wife and yeah, maybe I am. But she doesn't want that boat. She wants the money and the dig at me and she wants to prance around on it and look rich. That's kinda why I let the boat get into such a state of disrepair. Figured it would serve her right when she brought her fancy friends down to the marina to go out on her big boat and laugh at me to find a stinking, sinking, rotten mess of a boat sitting there.

"I know it sounds small and all, but she turned into a not so nice person with not so nice friends and I wouldn't mind screwing her just a little. Pardon my language."

"But what will happen when she finds out you gave it away? Won't you get in trouble?"

"Ahhh. That's the catch. How about I sell you the boat?"

'What?" Ned practically shouted. "You just said you would give it to her!"

"Whoa, whoa, Ned. Relax. You got five dollars, kid?"

"Well, not if I pay for this sandwich I'm eating."

"Okay, I'll buy you lunch. You give me five bucks and that's what I write on the bill of sale. A judge might be able to force you to surrender the boat if I just give it to you. But if you paid something for it, even five bucks, I think it makes it harder for anyone to mess with it. Legal sale and all."

Ned was nodding as Stan talked.

"Hmmm. So I guess it would be good if I sailed off into the sunset soon, eh?"

Stan started to laugh. "Oh, you got a good idea there, kiddo!" And he and Ned slapped the table and laughed and grinned at one another and at me.

"Hey, Lou Anne, bring the check. Stan's buying! And then we are going to go look at the boat he just sold."

"Be right with you, Ned."

"Hey, I thought you said you didn't know these guys," I said when she slid the bill onto the table.

"A girl gets to have some secrets, honey. You should know that!" And then it was all three of them laughing.

"Come on, girlie, show us your new boat."

"Well, it isn't exactly new, but I would be glad to show it to you."

So I walked back down the dock between the two old guys in hats to the *Mist B Haven*.

Chapter Thirteen

"Wow! She looks great, girlie! And no horrible smells come out when you open the salon door! In fact, it smells like a lemon orchard!"

Ned was content with the basic tour.

"I don't need to see greasy old engines. Might get some on my suit."

Stan wanted to see everything. He ran his hands along the polished rails and admired the way the mahogany had responded to cleaning and oiling. He stuck his head in the main state room and smiled. Everything was in its place. I showed him the cleaned V-berth with its four bunks all made up ready to be used. We pulled up the hatch and climbed down into the engine room. "Hey, Ned, there isn't any grease down here, your suit would be safe." He was clearly impressed with the state of the mechanics, all the tools stowed and the engines wiped down. He stuck his head into the bilge and chuckled. "Well, the pump is still working, but I've never seen such clean bilge water."

I was avoiding the upper deck, not wanting to go too near the captain's cabin. But Ned had climbed up while Stan and I had been below. He was laying out on one of the lounger chairs I had just found down the dock in the trash area. They were a bit faded and the cushions were a tad lumpy but with a little scrubbing and oil, my two go-to repair products, they were going to be a great addition to the boat. Finally, somewhere to sit!

"Boy, you have sure made this bucket look good," Ned said.

"Yep, you done real good, kid. She looks back to what she should look like. She has that live boat feel to her, live and happy."

"I think that too, Stan. She feels happy to me."

"Uh huh, and that is from all you have been putting into her. Boats are meant to be shipshape. I wasn't doing right by her, but you are. You really thinking of heading out?"

"I am. I was thinking of the Intracoastal towards Florida. Be gone before it gets too cold."

"Hmmm. You figure out how to run her? "

"I have. I had a good teacher and I think I'm ready."

"I saw your Coast Guard license on the wall in the salon. Good for you."

"Thanks, Ned. Yes, I did the course. It taught me a lot about boating and navigating and rules of the road. It gave me a pretty good start at understanding how to operate a vessel. And then I have been practicing docking and running in the open water and doing routine maintenance on the engines and pumps and stuff. The only thing I am still looking for is a refrigerator. The icebox works fine for when I am docked and can resupply every couple days. But I want to have a way to keep some stuff cold longer than a couple days. I have been asking around and hoping to find one before I head out."

"Well, that seems like a good idea...everyone wants their beer to be cold!"

"It's really about the food more than the beer," I laughed.

"Right."

"Hey, thanks for the tour, kid. Really, you have done a bang-up job on her. It makes me happy knowing she's in good hands. Got a captain that cares about her. Drop Lou Anne a postcard every now and then. She'll keep us posted on your travels."

"Stan, I can't tell you how much this means to me, you giving me this boat. You don't even know me! But I am so grateful."

"I didn't give it to you, you bought it. And I know you. I look around at this boat and I know you."

"I will think of you every day and I will be saying thank you for the rest of my life, Stan. Really, thank you, you have no idea what this means to me."

Stan was already halfway down the ladder.

Ned got up, settled his hat back on his head and gave my arm a friendly pat. "He has an idea girlie. That's why he did it." Then he followed Stan down the ladder and out onto the dock.

"Don't forget to write. Lou Anne can always find us." He waved and they both turned and walked back up the dock and out of the marina. I stood on the upper deck of my boat and watched them until I couldn't see them anymore.

Chapter Fourteen

I still had enough time to get to the Coast Guard office. It didn't seem like I needed to go now, but I had arranged with the clerk and I owed him two bucks. So I headed back up the dock to the CG Station. I found the right office and put a five-dollar bill on the counter.

"I think I owe some money."

"Ah yes, the owner search. Turns out I didn't really have to do anything. Guy came in this morning and changed the registration on the boat you were interested in. I noticed the numbers were the same right away. So here's a copy of the new registration. You might as well get something for your money." He handed me a single sheet of paper and three dollars change. I folded it all up and stuck it in the pocket of my khakis.

"Thanks."

"You want a receipt?"

"Nah, I'm good."

I retraced my steps back to the boat and went topside to sit on one of my "new" loungers. I dug the paper out and unfolded it. And there in block letters was my name on the new owner line. I was the legal owner of the *Mist B Haven*. I lay back and let the sun wash over me. I was warm from the inside out. My boat, my boat, I chanted to myself. She was my boat, but I felt like it would be a good idea to leave here sooner rather than later in case the ex-Mrs. Stan came looking.

I got up and went into the wheelhouse, pushed aside the charts I had been looking at and pulled out a piece of paper and began a list of provisions I would need to get on board before I could set out. First up was a wagon to carry my supplies in. Now that Alf was gone I would need my own. I needed to check with other boaters in the marina about buying a refrigerator. Maybe Billy, the dockmaster, would have a lead. I didn't want to eat just canned food. I wanted to have some fresh meat and vegetables and that meant something other than the icebox I currently had. I could start stocking up on dry goods, rice, beans, flour, oatmeal, salt, pepper, spices, coffee, tea, dried beef, powdered eggs, cans of milk, a couple cases of beer, potatoes, onions, soap that I could use for me and laundry and dishes, toilet paper. The list got longer and longer. The problem is, the more stuff I took the heavier the boat would be. The heavier the boat, the more fuel it would take to move her and fuel was weight, too. And of course at some point if I put too much stuff on board, I could sink her. But that wasn't very likely. Plus, the advantage to going down the Intracoastal was there were plenty of places to stop and resupply. Making the list got me excited about going. But it was too late to shop tonight. And shopping required money. And I didn't have any, except for three drawers full.

Chapter Fifteen

I got up and went into the captain's cabin. I slid the bolt in the door and pulled the curtain over the porthole. I didn't want anyone surprising me or watching either. I turned on the light and pulled out the top drawer. This was now my boat and maybe that made this my money. I doubted whose ever money it was would agree with me, but I at least wanted to know how much there was.

The money was just jammed in the drawer every which way. Some of the bills were all crumpled up, others, felt like they had gone through the wash, some had rubber bands around them. I straightened them all out and, sorted by denomination, it was mostly fifties and hundreds. There were a few smaller bills, but not many.

I decided to count each drawer separately. I would end up with three totals and one grand total. Drawer one had $47,280 plus the $420 I owed it. I put the stacks of sorted bills neatly back in the drawer. I repeated the same process with the second and third drawers. Drawer number two had $68,640 and drawer number three had $59,770. Grand total $175,690 + $420 brought the original total to $176,110. I just stared at the number. It seemed unreal until I opened a drawer and looked in. Then it seemed more than real. It was scary. What was I going to do with this money? It wasn't mine and yet, I had none of my own and right now, I needed to leave. Using this money was the only way I could.

I pulled out another sheet of paper and wrote the three drawer numbers at the top of three different columns. I put the total for each under that and then under drawer one I noted the $420 I had already used and subtracted, and then I wrote down $500 and subtracted. I stuffed the paper inside *Chapman's* and removed five one hundred dollar bills from the top drawer. This would hopefully cover the refrigerator, fuel and my growing list of supplies.

The five hundred bucks went in my pocket. I turned out the cabin light, slid the bolt back, opened the door and stepped out into a pitch-black night. I had lost track of the time. Counting money takes a long time, I decided. If it weren't so scary, it would have been fun. I climbed down to the main deck and went inside to get something to eat from the galley. A peanut butter and jelly sandwich and a lukewarm beer would have to be it for tonight. As I sat eating my sandwich, I began looking around. I would need to put that money somewhere other than stuffed in a drawer like it had been. I wanted somewhere hidden and safe to keep most of it. So far no one had questioned where my money came from, and I figured if I kept moving often enough, no one would. It isn't usually the first thing you ask someone. But I still wanted it hidden. Out of sight out of mind had been working so far. But I was rarely in the captain's cabin. If I began motoring, I would probably sleep up near the helm and not in my cabin down below, so it would be right there in front of me. I needed a hidey-hole. Soon.

Chapter Sixteen

I finished my sandwich and headed down to my cabin. I looked around for a hiding place in there and found nothing promising. I ruled out the V-berth since I might have guests someday and I didn't want them stumbling onto my money. Damn, not *my* money, *the* money. I needed to not think of it as mine yet. I needed to stay neutral. The engine room seemed like a good place. Stuff it up on one of the transom beams or behind the tools. When I looked, there were small spaces but none large enough to hide what I was trying to hide. I gave up for the night and went back to my cabin. As I was hanging my pants up I looked at the closet floor. Why not cut a hole and put a trap door that would blend in with the wood grain there? No one would be the wiser. The money could stay under the closet floor, close by and yet invisible, even to me. I was happy with the plan and slept soundly for the first time in a while.

I woke to a chilly rainy day. Perfect for what I was planning on doing. No one would be likely to be out walking the dock to see or hear anything, and a day inside would be a nice change. Once I had the hidey-hole made and the money safely stowed, I could curl up under a blanket and read or work on plotting a course to Florida. But, first things first. Coffee, breakfast, and then the day could start.

I kind of wished Alf were here to help me. But even if he had been, I couldn't really ask for help. Not for this. A hidey-hole is only as good as its hidey. Having someone else help build it kind of wrecks that. I went below to the engine room and got a knife-like Saws-All, some stain, sand paper and my go-to product, lemon oil.

I took all the clothes out of the closet and covered the bed with towels so the saw dust wouldn't make a huge mess. My plan was cut as close to the edge of the closet wall as I could, making the cuts blend in with the boards so no one would notice them. Once the floor planks were up, I would frame in the four sides, though probably only two, since the floor beams would serve as the other two sides. Create a bottom if the subfloor was too deep. Sand the hole edges and refit the floor planks to look as natural as possible. Stain and oil would help them blend. I would need to put a small notch in one side of the plank cover so I could slide a knife in and raise the hole cover.

I went up to the galley to get the last of the coffee, topped up my mug and brought it below with me. I found an old bandana and covered my nose and mouth, plugged in the saw and knelt down to start the cut against the right hand wall. The saw slipped in easily and barely bit into any wood. I pulled it out to check the blade. It seemed solid and had good teeth still. I set up again. And then I saw it. A small notch in the right hand corner. I went to the dresser and got a pocket knife. I slipped it into the notch and pried. The whole closet floor began to move up, just as I had planned. Only I hadn't done anything yet. This was someone else's hidey-hole. I pulled the floor away and peered down into the opening, More money. **Lots** more money! I crab-walked away from it and sat down heavily. Holy smokes was all I could say over and over again. Holy smokes!

The *Mist B Haven* sure seemed to be living up to her name.

Chapter Seventeen

Once my heart had stopped pounding I crawled back to the closet and looked again. Yep, still a lot of money down there. It was different than the stuff in the drawers up top. This was all neatly stacked in packets with rubber bands around them. I stuck my saw blade down into the hole to see how deep it was. The eighteen-inch blade totally disappeared. This hole was at least two feet deep. The hatch cover/floor panel was two feet by two and a half feet and the money was pretty much filling the hole. I pulled out one of the packets and counted it. $10,000 in hundreds. A second held the same. A third the same. At that rate there were several MILLION dollars lying in front of me. I couldn't even wrap my mind around it. I put the lid back on and tamped it down until no evidence it was there remained.

So someone else had had the same thought I did. How do I hide something on a boat? The problem for me, was I still needed to find a place to hide the money that remained in the drawers, and where the heck did all *this* money come from? The first problem was the most pressing, I still needed to hide the other money. So I decided to see if there was another place on board that I could cut a hidey-hole, since my first choice was already taken. I decided to try the captain's closet. I climbed back up to the upper deck and went into the small cabin. It was much smaller than my cabin but it was cozy. A built-in bed on one wall and a built-in bookcase and half closet with shallow drawers under it filling the opposite wall. Rats. I had forgotten that this closet didn't go all the way to the floor, the drawers did. More storage was built in under the bed. The third wall directly across from the door was a built-in desk or table actually. It had no drawers, just a desktop. So that is where I decided to create my floor safe.

Cutting into the floor was a bit awkward as I crouched under the desk. But at least no one else had sawed here before me! The space between the floor and the joists below was only 8 inches but that would be more than enough room for the drawer money. I decided to make the opening a foot square. That would give me plenty of room but the money wouldn't be sliding all over once we were underway. Once I had the hole complete and the edges sanded and oiled, I transferred the money into it. I slid the lid back in place and sat back to admire my handy work. Not bad, and unless you crawled around under the desk, you wouldn't see the notch or suspect that anything was out of the ordinary. I was happy and proud of my woodworking skills. I had been learning a lot of different things since I climbed aboard the boat nine weeks ago.

I knew I really needed to stock up and get out of here, even if only a day's sail down the coast. I needed to quit sitting here waiting for someone to show up and yank the rug out from under me. Action. I needed to get myself in gear, but the cold and the rain kept me inside curled up with hot chocolate and a book.

I spent the next few days shopping for provisions. I would fill my wagon with supplies, go back to the boat, unload, and head right back out. Groceries, the marine shop for extra oil, transmission fluid and filters, and a new rain slicker and pants in bright yellow. A pair of tall rubber boots finished off the outfit. I also purchased a second pair of sunglasses in case one pair went overboard. Being out on the water without sunglasses was a recipe for sunburned eyeballs and eye strain. Didn't need that. I stopped at the men's clothing shop and picked out a couple pairs of new khakis, a pair of jeans, two heavy wool sweaters, a packet of new tee shirts and three long sleeved cotton shirts. The clerk tried to sell me socks, but who needs socks when you rarely wear shoes! A warm Navy surplus pea coat was the last of my purchases.

I spent the evenings stowing everything I had bought during the day. The final project was finding a fridge. Once that was on board I would cast off. It felt good to have a plan.

Chapter Eighteen

The morning was sunny and warm, probably one of the last of those kind of days before the chill of fall really set in. I went down the dock to find Billy, the dock master, to see if he had any leads or ideas about a small refrigerator for my boat. If I couldn't find one today, I would give up on the idea for now and just keep using the icebox until I could find one, maybe at my next stop. I found him tipped back in a chair basking in the sun.

"Hey, Billy, do you know where I can get a real refrigerator for my boat?"

"What? No good morning or how's it going or how are you today? Nah, just jump in to whatever you got on your mind. Phhhffft, kids today. Got no manners."

"Sorry, good tip. I'll try to remember that. So how are you today?"

"Ah, forget it. Now you just feel obligated. Refrigerator for your boat. Don't you have one? "

"Yeah, but it's an old ice box not a real fridge. I kind of want to upgrade if I can."

"You want it to run on propane or electric?"

"Hadn't thought about it. Electric, I guess. I don't carry that much propane."

"You gonna put it in yourself?"

"Well, I was going to try, though I don't know that much about electrical systems."

"Personally, I wouldn't try it. Electricity can be a shocking thing. I would just buy a new fridge and have the guys come install it. You think you are going to save money with someone else's old fridge, but they usually got rid of it for a reason. You don't always know it till you get it all set up on your boat and it don't run. Very frustrating!"

"So you think I should just go buy a new one?"

"Nope, I think you should do what you want. I was just saying what I would do. I know that catamaran over there is replacing one, so you might want to go talk to them. Maybe they would be willing to sell it cheap. Or you can go out the gate, turn right and go down about two blocks to Handly and Sons and tell them I sent you. They'll be fair with you if you are fair with them."

"Thanks, Billy. I think I will go up and talk to them. See what we can arrange."

"Good choice. The cat's fridge is dead, but they would sell it to you anyway."

"Are you kidding me? And you would have let me go over there and buy it?"

"Live and learn, kid, live and learn."

That earned him a bit of a snort from me. He laughed and I went up the dock towards the gate.

"Remember to say good morning," he called after me.

"Got it. Lived and learned," I shouted back.

I could hear him chuckle as I got to the gate and turned right towards Handly and Sons.

The mention of Billy's name dropped the price twenty-five dollars and installation was half price. Delivery was scheduled for day after tomorrow. It meant I had to spend a couple more days in port. Now that I had decided to leave, I was anxious to get going. But I could use the time to lay in some fresh fruits and veggies to put in my new fridge and to plot my course on the new charts I was headed off to buy at the Coast Guard Station.

New charts in hand, I decided on a late lunch at the coffee shop. A couple more days and I would be cooking all my own meals. Might as well let someone else cook for me till then!

"Hey, Lou Anne." I sat down at an empty booth. I had my pick as the place was deserted except for two guys eating at the counter.

"What'll ya have today, hon?" she asked as she set a cup of coffee in front of me.

"Clam roll and fries would be great, thanks." She shouted the order through the window to the kitchen and turned back to top up the coffee of the guys at the counter.

I unrolled the first chart, leaned down close to it and took a deep breath. Even over the smell of coffee and fried food, I could still catch the faint scent of ink, good paper and maybe just a little bit of ocean, though that last part was probably my imagination. I traced a path from the marina out into the harbor and on past the breakwater to open ocean. I would be out in open water for a couple hours before I could tuck back in and start down the Intracoastal waterway. Alf and I had been out past the breakwater a number of times, practicing steering through the waves. It was fun. And even though this would be my first solo trip out, I felt pretty confident about it.

Lou Anne brought the clam roll and fries and set a bottle of ketchup on the table.

"I already had Gus put the cocktail sauce on the plate for you. I know you don't like the tartar."

"Thanks."

"You getting ready to head out?" she asked as she gestured towards the charts with her coffee pot.

"Yep, I think so. Maybe day after tomorrow."

"Huh. Well, you take care of yourself and send me a postcard if you get somewhere pretty."

"I sure will. Might send one even if it isn't real pretty."

She laughed, "Nah, I only want pretty," she said as she walked away. "Pretty is important."

I moved the chart over so there was room for my plate. I didn't want to get anything on it, at least not yet. Eventually it would have plot lines and coffee stains and what not, but I wanted to at least start out with a clean chart.

"Where you heading?" One of the guys at the counter asked.

"South."

"Hmm, how far south?" he got up and walked over to the table.

"I'm not sure yet, somewhere where it doesn't ice up, that's for sure."

"Well, this chart will take you to Georgia and those other two still rolled up over there will get you south of Florida. So where are you headed?"

I didn't like the tone this guy had and I didn't like how he was leaning over me with his hand on my nice clean chart.

"Like I said, I haven't decided." I started to roll up the chart, his hand didn't move.

"All by yourself? A girl like you? Don't you want a man around? I could go along and keep you company if you like. Could be real fun."

"I don't need or want your company. Now move your hand off my chart," I said in the steadiest voice I could muster.

"Oooh, don't want my company...what are you, some kind of dyke?"

Suddenly Lou Anne was at the booth holding a pot of hot coffee.

"You best be paying your bill and moving on. I don't care for that kind of talk." She stared at him hard and motioned towards the door with the pot. "I'll be right up to the register to cash you out. Go on now." She leaned in and poured a bit more coffee in my cup. The guy was clearly thinking about arguing. "You want this all down the front of you, you just open your mouth." Steam rolled out of the top of the pot. He moved his hand and walked slowly back to the counter.

"Come on, Danny. We don't need to hang around some lesbo burger joint." He threw three dollars on the counter and slammed out the door with his friend following.

"Now you just don't think nothing of that, hon. Guys like him can't stand the thought of a woman being by herself and being happy. And if they do think about it, they get all afraid they won't be important anymore. It kind of shrinks their balls, I think. Seeing some woman succeed without a man. You just keep on keeping on."

"Thanks, Lou Anne. I don't know what to say. That was creepy."

"That's why I always have a pot of hot coffee handy. You might do well to do the same." She smiled, patted me on the shoulder and walked to the counter to start cleaning up. "Well, what a surprise, no big tip from those guys."

I slid a ten-dollar bill under my plate. "I'll be sure to cover it."

Chapter Nineteen

I left the coffee shop but was too unnerved to go back to the boat. I wandered down the street looking in shop windows and scanning the street for those two guys. I wasn't sure why they unnerved me so much. Was it that it reminded me I was alone, or more to the point, a woman alone? Was it that they assumed if I didn't want their company I was a "dyke"? I wasn't sure I had ever heard that word before, but I knew instinctively what it meant. It seemed like a weird thing to say to someone. Just because I didn't want to invite a stranger to get on my boat and travel with me, I was a lesbian. I wouldn't invite a strange man to live in my house. Why should I invite him on my boat? It was my home.

I began to think about what I was doing, planning on traveling alone on a forty-eight-foot boat thousands of miles or even a hundred miles, with no one knowing where I was or where I was going. Including me in a way! I was nineteen, I hadn't seen the ocean until a year ago, I had never even set foot on a boat until ten weeks ago, and then, as it turned out, I stepped off its owner. I barely knew the general geography of the United States. The only two maps I had ever seen had the states and countries separated by different pastel colors. I had learned chart reading in a class! I had never set a course and followed it, not by myself. Alf used to pick a compass heading and I would steer towards it, but that wasn't really navigating. Everything I knew about my boat some man I barely knew taught me. I wasn't a lesbian, I was crazy!

The guy was right. Who did I think I was to try this alone?

I shoved my hands deep in my pockets and turned back toward the marina feeling small and defeated.

"Hey, hon!" Lou Anne was standing just outside the coffee shop waving a card. "The mail just came and you might want to read this." She shoved it into my hand. "You can take it. I already read it."

I looked down at the picture postcard in my hand. It looked like some big plantation house with moss hanging on all the trees, pretty in a spooky way. I flipped it over.

> *Hey Lou Anne! I made it to Savannah and am holed up here with a busted propeller and the flu. Kind of a bad combo. Sailing was smooth and all really is well. Got a new prop ordered, and the doc says the flu shouldn't last more than a couple days. I have been thinking of and missing you. Hope all is well. Tell the kid to quit lollygagging and get down here. I leave the end of the month. Get a move on.   Alf.*

Alf! I raced inside, grabbed Lou Anne and did a little dance. "Stop. Stop," she laughed, "People *will* talk now!" She still laughed.

"I can't believe he wrote me."

"Well, he didn't write you. Technically he wrote me."

"Yeah, I know but he sent a message to me. I know where he is and I can join him. He practically invited me!"

"He did invite you. I read the card too."

She saw both my excitement and my indecision and insecurity. "Look, hon, there are good ones and bad ones in the world. Hang out with the good ones as much as you can and with the bad ones as little as you can. It will lead to a pretty good life in the end is my experience."

She was right. All these years later I know she was right. I can still see her standing in the coffee shop doorway waving me off, her apron fluttering in the light breeze. "You be sure to tell him hello for me and write, darn it!"

Chapter Twenty

Now I could hardly wait to get underway. Alf's postcard had come at a perfect time. It was just the encouragement I needed. A destination and someone I knew at the end of the trip, provided I could get there by the end of the month.

I went up to the helm station. Filed the new charts in the long thin chart drawer and pulled out the old and new chart for the first leg of the trip. I stuck Alf's postcard next to the compass and began to plot the first leg of my trip south.

The new fridge was installed and humming away by eleven the next morning, and I was ready to be gone. I dropped the lines and eased the *Mist B Haven* out of her slip for the last time. I motored over to the fuel docks to top up the tanks. Billy grabbed lines but waited to tie them off.

"Fill her all the way up Billy, I am heading out and I want plenty of fuel!"

"How much you got in her right now?"

"She's at three quarters full, but I want to start out full."

"You got plenty to make Union Beach or Port Monmouth." He threw her lines back on board and shoved her nose out. "You best be going now, if you want to go at all." He nodded towards the marina gate. I could see several guys in dark suits and hats and a blond woman in a deep green dress and heels coming into the marina and looking at the now empty slip I had just pulled out of.

"Stan's ex?"

"Yup, and I wouldn't stay to say hello if I was you."

"Thanks, Billy, for everything."

I put the starboard engine in gear and put the *Mist B Haven*'s nose out into the marina basin, engaged both engines and began to motor slowly out towards the breakwater. I could hear shouting behind me. I turned and waved at Billy who was still on the dock. He was surrounded with suits. I could see the woman, hands on hips, staring out at me. She raised her hand in a gesture I had never seen a woman make. I waved back and pointed my bow to the open water.

Once I was out into the open sea, I set a course and throttled way back. Billy was right, I had plenty of fuel to get to the marina at Port Monmouth, but I hadn't planned to stop there. I would need to replot my course. It was slow going for me since I was new at it and I had to keep looking up to be sure I was headed in the right direction and that no other boat was in my vicinity. I eventually had a course and a new heading. I set the boat on the new course, throttled up and sat on the stool at the helm to watch the ocean pass under my bow. I was on my way!

It occurred to me as I sat and steered that maybe the ex-Mrs. Stan would figure out that I had been trying to fuel and would send someone to board me when I pulled in at the next logical fueling stop. I had legal title to the boat, I knew that for sure. I had put the registration in a frame right next to my Captain's License in the main salon. But I wasn't prepared for a long drawn out court battle, or even a short one. And there was still the "problem" of the enormous amount of money on board with no known owner. I doubted it was hers, since she seemed to have taken everything she could have off the boat.

Why would she take the sheets and leave a huge amount of cash? But I wasn't interested in testing my theory.

I pulled back on the throttles which slowed the boat, and once again, replotted a course, this time heading much farther down the coast. Three quarters of a tank should take me quite a ways. But since I hadn't really run the boat long distance I didn't have an accurate idea of how far exactly it would take me. Alf speculated at one point that I might start with an estimate of ten gallons per hour running at ten knots, which is about eleven miles an hour. That's without figuring in wind, current, sea height. In other words, it really was a very large ball park figure and underestimating meant running out of fuel.

I looked at the charts and set a course to run parallel to the coastline. I figured I could pull in towards shore at any point I got nervous or just decided to. I also realized I wasn't really prepared to run after dark, so that too would limit my range. It was mid-October; the sun was going down around six or six thirty. I wanted to be in port before it got dead dark. I would see where I was and what was nearby at around five. That gave me four hours and almost fifty miles more distance between me and the ex-Mrs. Stan. That seemed like a plan.

I motored back up and reset my heading away from Port Monmouth towards Atlantic City. This part of the journey was all in the open ocean. The Intracoastal Waterway was mostly inland but this first section out of Jersey City was open water till you got to the Manasquan Inlet around Brielle. That was where I was headed if I could get there before dark or running low on fuel.

The seas were relatively calm for this time of year, though there was a swell pushing my bow starboard towards shore. I corrected to the compass heading I had selected and began to relax. I enjoyed being out on the water, just me and the *Mist B Haven*. Birds and water and nothing. Perfect.

I could see the shore, I didn't want to run too far out and then have to turn back and motor in. I could see the channel markers for the Intracoastal and made the cut inland. These were more protected waters. I could navigate by the channel markers spaced along the way I didn't need the chart now, except to know which town I was passing. I was making good time so I passed the marina at Brielle and continued on to Shore Acres. I throttled back as I approached the fuel dock and looked around for someone that could be with Stan's ex, but laughed at myself. How would I even know. I needed fuel and this was where I could get some. An old bow legged guy came out from the fuel hut and tossed lines over the cleats on my bow and stern. Once I was snugged up to the dock I climbed down to the main deck.

"Need fuel?"

"Yep, both tanks need to be filled up."

He handed me the fuel hose and I opened the tank and stuck the nozzle in. "Fire away." I called. He cranked up the pump and the process began. Filling both tanks was not going to be cheap but I had raided the top drawer for cash and wasn't worried about total price. I *was* worried about the former Mrs. Stan. I didn't want to stay on land any longer than I needed to.

"Are you going to want a slip for the night or are you happy with a mooring?"

"Huh?"

"Well, a slip will cost you five bucks but you get water and electric, or you can pull up on one of those mooring balls out there for a buck. No power or water hook ups out there "

"No power is fine I'll take a mooring. Any one in particular?"

"Nah, you can have your pick tonight. Just be sure you put out enough scope so you don't pull the tackle up or break the line if it starts to blow."

"Gotcha."

I switched the fuel hose to the dock side of the boat. "Hey, can you watch this for a minute? I need to go below."

He gave me a funny look but said sure. I figured he must think I needed to pee or something. And that was fine with me. Really, I was headed for my copy of *Chapman's* that I had in my cabin. I pulled it out and opened to the mooring section. It showed exactly how to pull up on a mooring ball, how to fish the painter line out of the water and connect it to a line from my boat. And it explained scope which was the angle of the line attached from my boat to the pin or mooring ball. If the angle was too steep, the line too short, it would put strain on the mooring line and tackle pulling almost directly up on it. Not good. More line meant a gentler angle and less strain on the mooring and my own boat. I offered up a big thank you to whoever Chapman was. The book had saved me from asking what scope was or how to tie myself up. This was not the last time I would need to refer to the book to help me look like a boater and not some silly landlubber girl. Which, in fact, I probably was!

I went back topside more confident about what I was doing and the old guy was just finishing fueling. "Thanks for the hand." I paid for fuel and the one-night mooring fee and waited while he prepared to drop the lines.

"You want the bow or stern line dropped first?"

"Drop the bow first and I will back down on the stern."

Good" he said. His look seemed to show a bit more respect. At least I knew how to get off his dock.

"Bow's free."

"Hold the stern for my signal." I said. This is what Alf used to say to me I figured it must be okay to say to strangers.

I put the starboard engine in reverse and that pulled my bow away from the dock and pointed my nose out into the channel. "Okay, let her go." I called.

"Stern's free."

I engaged both engines forward and moved away from the dock. "Thanks a lot." I waved and moved out towards the line of mooring balls.

"Have a good night," he called.

Chapter Twenty-One

The trick with mooring when only one person is on board is that there is only you to do everything. I had to be quick on my feet and ready. I slowly approached the mooring and put the boat in neutral. Of course, momentum would keep me moving forward for a little bit. I raced out of the wheelhouse and skipped the ladder, jumping down from the top deck onto the bow. I had prepared a pole with a hook on the end. I would use this to reach out and grab the floating line attached to the mooring ball. I had also coiled a line on the deck to use to tie off with. I leaned over the rail and snagged the mooring line on the first grab, pulled it up and ran the line from my boat through the loop in the end. Then I tied off my line and waited while the boat floated back away from the mooring ball. I adjusted the line to give more slack so the scope would be right, I hoped. Climbed back up to the helm station and shut the engines down. I went back out to the top deck and sat down to watch the boat swing on the mooring, relived that I hadn't made a fool of myself. I knew people were watching me, the dock guy if no one else. I was glad I hadn't had to back up or go around to repeat the approach to get the line. So far so good. I laid back on the lounger and fully relaxed for the first time since I had left the marina in Jersey City.

I fixed dinner and took it up top to watch the sunset. It looked the same as it had yesterday, but a new location seemed to add something new to it. A different skyline or something. And this was the first time I had spent a night on the boat not tied up to a dock. I could feel the boat swing on the mooring and also feel the slight rocking that came with the motion of the moving water around me. It was soothing and I was in bed asleep within an hour of sundown. Of course that meant I was awake about the time it came up too. I didn't realize it then, but this was to become the rhythm of my life, the sun dictating sleep and wake times. But right then I was just happy to wake up on my own boat with a new day in front of me, and that too was to be my reaction for most of my life.

Coffee and breakfast in hand, I went up to the helm and looked at what the day might hold. The weather seemed clear though cool. Light breezes from the northwest would speed me along. I hopped down to the bow and dropped the mooring line. Scrambled back to the helm and engaged the engines to reverse away from the floating line and then forward to start my first full day running south to meet Alf.

I was surprised at how much traffic there was on the waterway. Somehow I thought it would be just small boats or slightly larger like me, but nope, there were tugs and freighters and yachts three times my size. Seemed like if it floated, it was on the Intracoastal this morning. I followed the red channel markers with the yellow square on them. The chart showed that the yellow squares marked the Intracoastal Waterway and the regular red and green markers noted the actual channel. There were a lot of channels that turned off the main waterway. I didn't want to take any detours, so I paid attention to the yellow squares and the chart just to be sure I was going where I wanted to go.

The next couple days passed fairly easily as I ran along inside the barrier islands of New Jersey. The lights of Atlantic City were quite beautiful to see one night. Shining out across the water. I would need to make a decision by the time I got to Cape May. I either turned inland for real and stayed on the Intracoastal up north through the Chesapeake Bay or I could head out into open water and skirt the shoreline of Delaware, Maryland and Virginia before picking the waterway up again in North Carolina. The problem with being in the open water was I couldn't just stop to sleep. I would need to stay awake and steering the whole time. The problem with the inland route was it would take me much longer and was miles out of my way. I wanted to get to Savannah before Alf left, but I knew I couldn't stay awake the two to three days it would take me to skirt the coast. So that made my decision. Inland I would go.

Chapter Twenty-Two

Turned out to be a lucky decision on several fronts. A tropical storm was blowing across the Caribbean and that made the seas rough and it eventually came on up the coast to the Carolinas. I would have been out in high seas with winds blowing more than 50 mph. I was happy to be tied up high in the Chesapeake Bay when that weather blew by. And because I was tied up, I gained a traveling companion.

I was just pulling off the fuel dock in a small marina outside Annapolis when I saw a guy carrying a burlap sack down the dock. Whatever was in the sack was moving around and as he passed my boat I could hear yowling. He heaved the sack out into the boat basin "Too damn many cats around here. They steal your catch when you turn your back. Tired of them robbing me."

I couldn't stand the thought of deliberately drowning animals for any reason, even if it were a good one. I motored over towards where he had thrown the bag and hopped down to the main deck. Got my gaff out and tried to snare the bag before it sank. It took me two shots, but I finally managed to hook it and pull it up out of the water and towards my boat. Once it was on the deck I quickly cut the top open and dumped it on the deck. Three kittens and what was probably the momma landed on the deck. None moved. "Bastard. Damn bastard!" I flung the empty bag over the side "What the hell is wrong with you?" I shouted at the now departed man. I slumped down on the wet deck and cried. It seemed so cruel.

"Hey, watch your boat!" someone shouted. I looked up and realized I had been floating towards several other boats resting at anchor. I jumped up and ran for the helm. I got there in time to engage the engines and miss hitting either boat, but only barely. It was the first time I had forgotten I was on a moving thing and that I needed to control it at all times, even if I was upset. I found a small bay and pulled in, dropped my anchor and backed down on it to secure it on the bottom. Once the boat was secure I went back down to the main deck to clean up the mess. I figured I could swim ashore and bury the cats inland a bit. When I got back to where they lay, one of the kittens was moving. It had its eyes open and was trying to crawl over to its mother. None of the others moved. They had been in the water too long. I picked the lone survivor up and made a cradle out of the bottom of my tee shirt. I took it inside and got a towel from the galley. I dried the little thing off as best I could. It looked so tiny. I got a can of milk down, opened it and soaked a washcloth with it. I put the kitten, wrapped in a towel, in the sink in the galley and placed the washcloth near its head. It began to sniff at the milk soaked cloth and then began to nurse.

I left it there while I gathered up the bodies of the other two kittens and the mother cat and wrapped them in a towel. I could have dropped them into the water and let the sea take them, but it didn't seem right. They deserved to be buried on land and not in the water that killed them. I took a small hand shovel and the now full towel, slipped over the side of my boat and swam to shore. Half an hour later I was swimming back with just the shovel. I climbed onto my boat shivering. A nice warm shower would help me wash off the cold and hopefully the sorrow. I found the surviving kitten still wrapped in the towel, sleeping in the galley sink where I had left it. I picked up the whole bundle, careful not to wake it, carried it in and laid it on my bed. That's where I found it five minutes later when I emerged from the shower, warmer, if not happy. I slid into bed and pulled the kitten close to me. It mewed in a semi-awake way and curled into me. I nodded off and awoke sometime later that night to the sound of a tiny motor running right next to my ear. That cat ended up sleeping on my pillow most nights for the next seventeen years.

I stayed at anchor most of the next day, feeding the kitten with the milk soaked washcloth and trying to figure out if I could keep a cat on board. It didn't seem like a very wise choice. So much could go wrong, most of which ended with cat overboard. But I liked having another living thing on board. I hadn't realized I was lonely, and I wasn't really. It was just kind of nice to have something to talk to, even if it was a kitten.

"Okay, so we agree, you're staying but you are going to live inside, no wandering around out on deck, right?" She looked at me barely lifting her head. "And I will have to figure out a litter box and food for you. And a bed, you are not sleeping next to my ear again!" This time she didn't even open her eyes. I made a list of supplies I would now need to add to my usual shore shopping list. I would need to do the shopping soon if I wanted to keep my boat clean and sweet smelling.

I decided not to go back to the marina where she had been tossed in the water. I was afraid of what I might do if I saw that guy again. I left her curled up in a blanket on my bed and went about making preparations to pull anchor and head farther south. Fair Haven seemed like a good spot to pull in and resupply. I tied off at the day dock and checked in with the dock master. He gave me directions to the nearest grocery and marine supply store and said I was welcome to stay tied off on the dock for two hours. I hoped that would be enough time to get everything I needed. I hurried down the dock pulling my wagon behind me. It took almost the whole two hours to get everything on my list. On my way back to the boat I saw a pet shop so I stopped in to pick up a collar, a cute ceramic food bowl and a small shallow wicker basket with a red plaid cushion. A perfect cat bed.

Wagon stuffed, I returned to find several people standing on the dock near my boat. "Something sounds pretty mad in there." One of the guys said nodding towards the cabin. I stopped and listened. And yes it sounded like something was pretty mad. There was a good amount of screeching and occasional sounds of things falling.

"Uh Oh." I muttered under my breath. "Yeah, I have a new mate and I'm not sure how it is going to work out." I sort of chuckled as I climbed on board.

"Well, it doesn't sound promising," the guy chuckled back.

"Nope, it sure doesn't."

Chapter Twenty-Three

I went into the salon and down to my cabin. The volume was definitely increasing. "Hey," I said as I opened the door. "What the heck is going on in here. Holy smokes, you sure can make a mess little one!" A pair of green eyes blinked down at me from the top of the closet door. And the loud meowing continued. "For such a tiny thing you can really crank up the volume. Here, let me get you down from there." I reached up and plucked her off the door top, sat down on the bed and set her in my lap. "Shhh, it's okay. I should have told you I was leaving. Shhh, I am back now. All right?" She began to knead my leg with her little paws. The meowing turned to purring. I looked around my cabin. She had pulled most of the books out of the bookcase, twirled the bed clothes into a major mess, pulled several shirts off their hangers and I think she peed in my high heel. Not that I would probably ever wear them again. Now I definitely wouldn't! Once I got her calmed down, I went back up on the dock to unload the wagon and stow it and my supplies away.

The same guy was still standing on the dock. "I had a dog once. Sailed with me for a couple years. Liked to stand on the bow and bark at the waves. Goofiest thing you'd ever want to see. He'd jump in the water and swim around the boat. He was a good little swimmer too."

I was afraid to hear the answer but I had to ask, "What happened to him?"

"He got too old to be safe on the boat so I gave him to my daughter. She and her kids would take him to the ocean and he would run up and down the beach barking at the waves. Made everyone laugh. Died in his sleep at twelve."

"Sounds like a good life."

"Yep, I reckon. You had that cat in there long?"

"Since yesterday."

"Well, she might be seasick, not all animals can adjust to the boating life."

"Hmmm, I think she was just startled to wake up alone in a strange place. Hopefully she won't get seasick. I never thought of that."

"Well, good luck to you and the kitty. Just remember, dogs can swim, cats not so much."

"Right. Thanks." And he was right. Cats not so much. I was going to have to find a way to be sure that the cat had plenty of room to move and places it could go on the boat without risking it sliding overboard. If I kept the salon doors closed, that would keep her off the back deck and she could wander around in the salon and galley and below in my cabin and the V-berth. The helm station and captain's cabin were going to be off limits till I figured out a way for her to move between them without going outside. At first blush it seemed mean to keep her inside, but then I thought of all the cats who happily lived in small apartments and never went out. I figured she would have way more space than many apartments. She wouldn't need to come to the helm, but I kinda liked the idea of her company when I was running the boat. I could imagine her curled in her bed on the chart table.

I went back inside and down to my cabin. She was sitting on the bed looking at the door. "Hey, no worries, here I am." I stooped to pick up an arm load of books to reshelf. "Boy, you made a mess in here little one. I guess you don't like being left alone, huh? Well don't worry, for the most part I am here. I just get off to get groceries and fuel. And to get you this excellent little collar." I slipped it over her head. "This way everyone will know that you are not a stray, that you have a home and a person."

I went back out and headed up the stairs to the salon. "Come on little one, come up top with me." I heard her jump down from the bed and wander out into the companionway. "Come on, let's go upstairs. Uh oh, your little legs might not make it up the stairs quite yet." So I picked her up and set her down in the salon.

It wouldn't be a week before she was flying up and down the stairs, no problem. And by then I had figured out how to cut a hole in the ceiling of the galley that opened into a cupboard in the wheelhouse and another hole through the wall of the wheelhouse into the captain's cabin which allowed her full access to every indoor part of the boat. She could jump to the top shelf in the galley and then climb through the hole to the wheelhouse. As she grew, it got easier and easier for her to maneuver this until I think neither she nor I thought about how she went from one place to another at all.

Chapter Twenty-Four

I think her initial experience with water made her happy not to go out near it. And really as long as she could be where I was, she was content. And so was I.

I put the new wicker bed up on the ledge at the helm. The ledge ran all the way across the cabin under the front windows. I usually set my coffee cup and whatever chart I was using on it. The copy of *Chapman's* held a place there. But there was still plenty of room for the little bed and she seemed to like to sleep curled up in it with the sun on her as we motored along towards Georgia.

"I can't keep calling you little one since you won't be for much longer! So what shall we call you? Hmm? You got a name?" Barely a head raise. "Sleepy head? Napper? Kitty?" I had been trying out names all morning but none of them seemed to fit her. "Maybe I'll just call you No Name. Or Cat. Though I think people who name animals Dog or Horse are unimaginative and somewhat impersonal. Don't worry, I won't name you Cat." Still barely an ear flick. I turned back to study the chart and make sure we were still on course. She hopped up, stretched and disappeared into the cupboard. "Fine, be that way. I can navigate without your help."

I found a small cove where I could drop anchor and fix lunch, maybe have a little nap. I went below to make some soup and found yet another mess. This kitten was just that. A kitten. She had a ton of energy and not a lot of sense. She was sitting on the floor in a puddle of chocolate syrup, her face covered in the dark brown sticky stuff. She had knocked the plastic bottle off the counter where I had left it after squirting some into my third cup of coffee. She had pulled the lid off and now sat in the middle of a chocolate sea.

"Well don't you look a fright." but I couldn't help laughing. I would have to learn to put things away after I used them. Not just because of her, but I realized I was still thinking like a person who lived on land. At any moment my house could rock or roll and loose items could become lethal as they flew off counters or shelves. "Okay, good lesson for both of us. But now I need to get you cleaned up. You are one big ball of Bosco!" And there was her name. Bosco. She didn't like the bath, but I think she liked the sticky stuff all over her even less. By the time I had cleaned her and the galley up and had a bowl of soup it felt like a full day. I looked at the charts and figured I would have ten more days of cruising to get to Savannah, at my current pace. That seemed still possible, but I needed to not dilly-dally. I was just looking for a reason to stop and play. Nope. Keep going. So I hoisted the anchor and motored back out into the main channel to get four more hours closer to my destination. Discipline didn't come naturally to me, but I was learning. If I didn't want to miss Alf, I would need to keep going I could stop and play, but then I might miss my friend. Choices were everywhere, but so were the consequences. The still damp and newly named Bosco crawled into her bed and settled in for an extended tongue bath. "Oh what, I didn't do a good enough job? Or are you just trying to get the last taste of chocolate? We are moving, Gotta get more miles in today. Wait till you meet Alf.

Boy, will that be a surprise for both of you! I don't know what he will think of having an animal on board. Hope he isn't allergic." I laughed. I could see him sitting up top in a lounger sneezing away! Time would tell.

Chapter Twenty-Five

I had pretty much stopped worrying about Stan's ex or her representative showing up and trying to claim the boat. I guess it was possible, but the farther I got from Jersey City, the less likely it felt. Still, I was happier either paying for a mooring or dropping anchor overnight. Being tied off at a dock wasn't appealing to me. I had had several run ins similar to the one in the coffee shop, men trying to invite themselves aboard, even if just briefly. So far I had managed to avoid any real trouble, but the fact that I was traveling alone, a single woman, drew the kind of attention I didn't want. So I stayed out on the water where I could hear someone approaching and not suddenly find some stranger stepping onto my boat from the dock. I was careful, but some nights I slept less well than others. I had taken to putting bags of empty cans on the back deck at night so if someone did climb aboard the chances were they would kick one of them and cause a racket. My homemade early warning system. It worked fine unless the seas were rough in which case I didn't put them out. No sense in creating false alarms and, if the seas were rough, nobody was rowing out to my boat. At least I hoped they weren't.

Bosco was turning out to be both good company and a major annoyance. She continued to wreak havoc on my living space. I had never had a kitten that lived inside before, only barn cats. So kitten behavior was all new to me. She especially liked climbing up things and usually in the process she would pull something down. The sheets off the V-berth bunks, charts from off the table, and her favorite, all the books from my cabin bookshelves. She had been on board a week or so and was growing quickly, which just seemed to aid her in her destruction. One evening I went below to get ready for bed and found every book on the floor and several with torn pages, victims of kitten rage, I guessed. Or boredom.

"Dammit Bosco, tossing the books on the floor is one thing, but chewing them up is a whole other deal."

She peeked out over the edge of the top shelf, green eyes blinking innocently. "Come on, get down from there so I can put everything back." I picked her up and set her on the bed and began gathering up the books and putting them away. Most of them had come from a second-hand book store Alf had introduced me to.

"Time can drag when you are on a boat sometimes, kid. Having a way to entertain yourself is a good idea."

So I had traded in most of the ones with the racy covers from the V-berth and stocked up on ten cent paperbacks and twenty-five cent hardcover books. I tried to pick a range of topics instead of just nonfiction or who-done-its. I had a good collection of things to read and most had survived the kitten onslaught undamaged. The log book had landed awkwardly and the spine was damaged and pieces of its pages were scattered on the floor. I gathered them up and put them on the bed. "Don't even think about touching these." I threatened with a finger point and a stern tone. The rest of the books were replaced and I finally had restored order. I sat on the bed and began to put the pages back in the log. I had stopped reading it weeks ago when it got repetitive and boring. Stan would write short entries like "motored south an hour and then back to the marina. "Sometimes he would list the passengers but usually not. I got tired of reading the same thing over and over. His entries weren't like Alf's which seemed to bring to life each voyage. I had started a new log that I was keeping at the helm station. I tried to make my entries less like Stan's and more like Alf's, writing about what I saw or felt or noticed as well as the facts of fuel consumption, repairs, where I was and where I was headed. I had pretty much forgotten about this one.

The pages were crumpled from their fight with Bosco. I tried to smooth them out before replacing them in the book. I noticed one of the pages wasn't in Stan's handwriting. In fact, when I looked more closely it wasn't from this log. The paper wasn't the same. Similar, but not the same. I wasn't sure where it had come from. Maybe it fell out of one of my other books. Someone else's bookmark.

"Hey, where did you get this one from?" I asked a sleeping cat. No answer. I smoothed it out on the bed and began to read it.

Seas are very rough, not sure the boat will hold together. Getting heavy water over the bow and the bilges are not keeping up with it. Wind screen has holes and next major wave will probably take it out. Can't hold a course, just trying to steer into the waves and take on as little water as possible. I suggested dumping the cargo but was overruled. If we keep taking on water, I will have to insist. Dumping it may be the only way to save the boat and everyone on it. We are definitely wallowing and partly that is the added weight. Sets us low in the water and tonight that isn't really a good place to be. Money can't buy good fortune. I wish I had remembered that.

The entry wasn't dated so it wasn't clear when this was happening or to whom. I wasn't totally sure it was about the *Mist B Haven*. No boat was named and the entry was unsigned. "Really, Bosco, where did this come from?" There wasn't another log on the shelf and the one that was there just had Stan's and Alf's entries. I had paged to the front and it appeared to started the day Stan bought the boat. That was why I felt like it was okay to start a new one myself. So where had this come from? I went over to the bookshelves and even though I knew every book and had placed them all back on the shelf just ten minutes ago, I looked again to see if there was some book I had missed, something that this page could have come out of. Nothing. "Boy, I wish you could talk." One green eye opened to look at me. "Any clues?" Nothing. I was tired and there didn't seem to be an easy answer tonight, so I turned off the lights and crawled in with the kitten.

Chapter Twenty-Six

Morning brought no new answers. I was beginning to believe it was a bookmark out of one of the other books and had nothing to do with the *Mist B Haven*. But that phrase, "Money can't buy good fortune." It stuck with me. But it wasn't true for me, money had bought me good fortune or at least paid the fuel bill so I could keep motoring on. How fortunate was that? And I was standing on my own boat and home. Mine, how fortunate was that? So far, I would say fortunate was my middle name. And I knew it.

I fixed coffee and a couple pieces of toast and went topside to check the weather and set a course for the day. I figured another five or six days and I would be in Savannah having a beer at sunset with Alf. I might be close enough in three days to get him on the radio late at night when reception was good. I would start trying then. Just to let him know I was close and coming on. I hoped he didn't leave before I got there. It would be close.

I pulled the anchor and headed out into the channel. Bosco clambered up from below and hopped up next to me, looking out at the water in front of us.

"So, I am going to need to fuel today and pick up a few supplies. I'll probably stop at lunch time so I can maybe find some food that I haven't cooked. I am sick of soup and sandwiches. I am looking forward to some french fries. Need a little grease in my system. Maybe I will bring you a piece of fresh fish if I see any. That could be good, huh?" She purred and rubbed against my hand. "I'll take that as a yes. But you only get treats if you don't tear the place apart while I'm gone. How is that for a deal?" More purring and rubbing. "Yeah, you are a real love bug, aren't you?" She left me to steering and curled up in her bed for a nap in the morning sun that was streaming through the windows, warming the cabin. I shed my sweater and drove on in shirt sleeves. This heading south was definitely a good idea. Warmer was always better as far as I was concerned.

I pulled into the marina at Pamlico Beach, which was about halfway down the coast of North Carolina. We were making good time. One of the guys standing on the dock looped the lines over *Mist B Haven*'s bow and stern cleats. "Why are there always guys standing on the dock? Don't they have jobs? They can't all be working at the fuel pumps." No answer from the sleeping cat. "What a hard life you have. It may have started out bad but it has definitely picked up since I fished you out of the drink." A yawn and recurl was my only response. "Fine. I'm going ashore. Do not cause trouble while I am gone." I opened the top drawer where I kept an envelope with cash in it. I didn't like just leaving it open in the drawer and when I was tied up, I didn't want to be seen opening my hidey-hole to get money. So I kept enough for a couple fuel stops and re-provisioning trips in an envelope and restocked it when I was offshore away from prying eyes. I stuffed the money in my jeans pocket. "Really, I mean it. Try not to make a mess for me to come home to." Ear flick.

I stepped outside the cabin and reached back in for my sweater. The breeze was a bit chilly and the sun hadn't heated up the outside nearly as much as it had the inside. I climbed down to the main deck and onto the dock. "Can I get fuel?" I asked the guy who tied me off.

"I reckon. You want it now or are you going into town first?"

"How long can I stay tied up here?"

"Couple hours. We aren't that busy and I have a couple long fuel hoses, so no worries."

"Great. Is there a place I can get groceries nearby?"

"Turn right out of the marina and head up Shore Street. There's a Winn-Dixie and a package store for liquor a couple blocks up."

"How about somewhere to get a burger?"

"Yep, this side of the Winn-Dixie, there's Buddy's Burgers."

"Any good?"

"I eat there every day."

"Well then, that sounds like a recommendation. Thanks. I'll be back in less than two hours."

Chapter Twenty-Seven

I untied the red wagon and pulled it down the dock towards Shore Street. I wanted to shop first and then eat, but I didn't want to go back to the boat to unload the supplies and I didn't want to have to watch a wagon full of stuff get warm while I ate. So lunch first it was. Buddy's had a local diner feel. I sat down at the counter and waited while everyone got through looking me over and went back to their lunches.

"What'll you have?"

"The Buddy Burger Basket would be great, thanks."

"To drink?"

"Cola if you got it."

"Just be a few minutes."

I nodded and swiveled around on the stool to look out at the street while I waited.

"I seen you come in. That your boat?" The guy next to me was hunched over a red plastic basket of food, but he managed to talk around a mouth full of burger.

"Yes, it is."

"Huh, I seen it down here before, but you weren't on it. Been a couple, five years though. You probably wasn't big enough to see over the wheel then. But there weren't no kids that I remember. Plus, the hoods on board didn't look like fathers."

"You've seen my boat before?"

"That's what I just said." He picked up a wad of fries, drowned them in ketchup and stuffed them in his mouth.

"Are you sure?"

"You invent that name on her stern? *Mist B Haven*?"

"No That was her name when I got her."

"Well that's how I know. Remembered the name and the look of her. Nice looking boat with the helm up top. Kinda awkward if you are single handling her, but you can see good from up there."

"Were you on board her then?"

"Yep, fixed a bilge pump for the guy claimed to be the captain. What kind of captain can't fix their own bilge pump? Unless they's a girl maybe." He gave me a look out of the side of his eyes.

"I can fix the bilge pump." I felt compelled to say.

"Didn't say you couldn't. But that fancy pants sure couldn't. They pulled up to the dock with about three feet of water sloshing around down there. Another couple hours and it was going to be a salvage operation." He snickered and I guessed he would have gladly done the salvaging if he got the chance.

"When was this?"

"Like I said more than five years ago. I still had my fingers then." He held up his right hand waggled his thumb and four stumps at me. "So that would be at least seven years."

I wanted to ask what had happened to his hand but I wanted to know about my boat more and I guessed it was either one or the other. "So you fixed the bilge. Can you tell me anything else?"

"Hell, I can tell you lots but I reckon you mean about your boat."

"Yes, about my boat."

"Not much else to tell. There were four or five wiseguys sitting in the salon smoking and playing cards when I came in. The "Captain" led me below to the bilge and showed me the water and busted pump. He told me they'd pay me a hundred bucks to fix it in less than an hour. I allowed as to how I could probably do it. Wasn't a damn thing wrong with the pump that a quick reconnection of the positive wire wouldn't fix." We both laughed. "But I didn't want him to know that and stiff me the money so I tinkered around with it while he stood in the companionway and smoked. After about fifteen minutes, I fired it up and it started pumping all that water out. He took me back up to the salon and one of the guys sitting there reaches in his pocket and pulls out a wad of bills. They all looked to be hundreds. He peels one off and hands it to me. 'Double or nothing?' he says. "Why, you got another bilge pump ain't workin?" I says "No," he says, "I got a cracked windshield and a pantywaist of a captain who claims it's dangerous to drive it like that. Think you can fix that in the next forty-five minutes?" "Nope," I says, "just give me the hundred for the bilge and we are square." But the guy won't let it go. He gives me the hundred and then says how about I fix it for two hundred more? "Show me the windscreen," I says."

"So now both the captain and Mr. Money are walking me up top to the helm station. The captain is trying to explain why sailing with a busted screen can be dangerous. Mr. Money looks at me and says, "Is that right?" "Yep. If you take a good wave over the bow and the water hits a cracked windscreen, it can break it in two and then you have water all over the helm, and wind and weather, too, if there is any. The man driving won't be able to see anything and with your bilge system, I wouldn't want to be taking a bunch of water in through the helm."

"He shows me the windscreen, says "Can you fix it?" "Yes sir, I think I can. I would need to go get a new piece of glass but it shouldn't take more than an hour." "Make it forty-five minutes and you get four hundred." As you can imagine, I took two quick measurements and was flying off that boat to get a piece of glass faster than a rabbit at the dog track. I finished caulking it in with about two minutes to spare. Mr. Money gave me the four hundred bucks and I hightailed it outta there. But that's how I know what your helm station looks like. I been in it."

He wiped the last of the ketchup and grease off the paper in the basket and licked his fingers. "Funny thing was, that weren't no cracked windscreen. It was three bullet holes made a mess of it. Still, could have popped if they took a wave, but I think they just didn't want to drive around with bullet holes showing like that." He chuckled. "Not that I blame them or anything. Holes like those do draw attention."

I had been eating my meal while he told his story. The burger was good and the fries were crisp and a bit greasy in a good way. But I hardly noticed the food. "So, how do you get bullet holes in a windscreen?"

"A gun," he snorted.

"Yeah, I know a gun. But who would shoot at a boat? And why?"

"Must have pissed somebody off. Plus, I thought I had seen the money guy before. Took me a while but I finally remembered seeing a picture of the guy being deported in the late 40's. It was Lucky Luciano handing out hundred dollar bills to the likes of me. Gave me the heebie jeebies when I figured it out. I could have just as easily been swimming with the fishes as stuffing hundred dollar bills in my pocket."

"Lucky Luciano?"

"Yeah, you know, the mob boss."

"But if he was deported, how was he back in the US?"

"Boats are beautiful things. They float around in the water and can pick up anyone. Just forget to tell customs and claim you never left U.S. waters, and maybe you didn't. Some folks call it smuggling, though no one around here does. We mostly call it making a living." He laughed in a sly kind of way and got up. "You got a nice boat, young lady. Just hope no one "cracks" your windscreen mistaking you for the former owners."

And off he went leaving me hoping the same thing, and wondering about money and good fortune.

Chapter Twenty-Eight

I paid for the burger basket with what could possibly be Lucky Luciano's money and turned towards the Winn-Dixie for groceries. I thought about stopping at the package store to pick up a bottle of something for Alf. But other than beer I had never seen him drink anything else. So I skipped it and went right into the grocery. It didn't take long to fill my wagon and head back towards the dock. When I got there, I could see a small group of men standing near the *Mist B Haven*. None of them looked extremely friendly, but it might have just been the heat of the sun on their dark hats and suits. Feds or wiseguys as the diner mechanic called them. I wasn't sure which was worse.

"Pardon me, excuse me." I tried to make my way through them with the wagon, careful not to bark any shins or roll over any toes. I pulled up to the stern and began loading groceries onto the gunwale.

"This your boat?" one of the suits asked. It seemed to be a popular question. I was used to people just assuming it was and refraining from asking.

"Yep." I kept on loading, not looking up to see who had spoken. It didn't really matter. They all wanted to know the answer.

"Owned it long?"

"Nope." I was playing it tight lipped. Answer the questions but offer nothing extra till I figured out what this was about.

"Hey, I'm talking to you." I looked up to see a small man surrounded by much bigger men. It was the smaller one who was 'talking' to me".

"No, you are asking me questions that aren't really any of your business as far as I can tell, and I am trying to load in these supplies so I can shove off."

"Well, let my boys help you." I could see this was going to be a problem. I didn't want any of these men on the boat because once they were, I wasn't sure I could get them off.

"I'm just finished." I said as I hopped on board and reached for the short hooked gaff I kept under the rail at the stern to haul in fish when I caught them. I knew in the face of a full attack it was relatively useless, but it might give some of them pause. "I don't know who you are or what you want. And I'm not sure I care. But the first man who steps on board could well lose an eye."

The man looked at me and a slow creepy smile spread over his face. "Well, well, well. The young lady has a feisty streak. I kinda like that." He turned towards his men. "Which of you wants to 'lose an eye' to the little lady here?" They laughed and jostled each other and began to goad the youngest one into trying it.

"Go on, Carlo, you afraid of a girl?"

"Come on, the worst that happens is we start calling you Blind Carlo!" That one got a good laugh.

They started pushing him forward closer to the boat. There wasn't much I could do but wait and hope some kind of help showed up. I doubted that was likely. But this was North Carolina not New Jersey, so maybe.

"Look, I don't want any trouble. I just want to drop my lines and go."

"Once we're on board you can drop a couple of other things, too," the little man smirked. "Come on, Carlo. What are you waiting for? You afraid of a girl?"

"I ain't afraid of no girl. It just don't seem right picking on a girl. My momma would be ashamed of me. I ain't afraid, I just don't think it's right. She's just a slip of a thing and I got at least hundred pounds on her. Ask her your questions from here. I ain't shaming my momma just so's you can scare a girl. One of you boys can, but I ain't. Ask her what you want so we can go."

There was some grumbling but no one stepped forward. The small man was suddenly not in charge anymore and he knew it. "You will pay for this you little bastard," he hissed at the much bigger man. "People do what I tell them."

"Yeah, they do, but that might be a problem. Ask your questions, Frank, and let's go." He motioned with his head towards the cars at the curb and most of the other men walked towards them. He leaned in to the smaller man who backed up a step before he caught himself and stood his ground. "I'm not afraid of a girl, and I'm not afraid of you, Frank. Those boys ain't loyal to you. They do what you say because Anastasi told them to. And now I think they will do what I tell them to. So no, you don't scare me. We done here?"

I waited. Still holding the gaff.

"We need answers," the guy named Frank whined.

"Fine." The big man turned to me. He had turned from a poorly-spoken hood to a well-spoken businessman in the space of less than a minute. "You own the boat, right?"

I nodded.

"For how long?"

"A couple months."

"Where'd you get it?"

"A guy in Jersey City sold it to me."

"Get a good deal?"

"Yeah, I did."

"He tell you anything about this boat?"

"Nope, just to be careful of the bilge pump 'cause it fails every now and then."

"Yeah, I heard that about boats." Frank blanched a little but kept quiet. The big fellow turned to him. "You got anything else you want to know?" He looked like he wanted to say something, but changed his mind. "Good, now let's go."

He nodded at me and smiled. "You might think about keeping a shotgun under that rail instead of some little hook. Way scarier and much more efficient."

I nodded back. "Good tip, thanks"

He turned and followed Frank up the dock to the waiting cars. He got in the front seat and a guy closed his door and ran around to the driver's side. Power changed that quickly. I went into the salon and collapsed on the couch. "Thank God for mothers!" I said to the curious cat at my side. "Thank God for *that* man's mother!"

Chapter Twenty-Nine

I sat for a couple minutes to be sure that my "guests" were gone and to give myself time to stop shaking. The adrenaline had certainly kicked in and it left me with the shakes. After a bit I went out to the stern to retrieve and stow the packages I had left there. The normal activity of the dock had resumed. I hadn't realized how quiet it had been while Frank and his muscle were here. A young kid stopped to see if I still wanted fuel.

"Yes, I do. Both tanks."

He pulled the hose to the port side tank and started pumping. "You got some interesting friends." He kept his head down while he offered his comment.

"Not friends. You know how they knew I was here?"

"Nope." Head still down.

"Huh. 'Cuz it sure seems strange that they would show up here out of the blue. Quite the coincidence."

"I reckon."

"Would ten bucks change your story?"

"Might do. You got ten bucks?"

"Might have. Tell me the story first."

"Well, I'm not saying this is what happened or nothing, but it might have happened that someone left some money to be called if this boat ever showed up."

"And who would someone call?"

"Don't know, just some number."

"Huh. Interesting. Did they pay for anything else?"

"Like what?"

"Like sabotage."

"Hell, I don't even know what that word means."

"Okay, sugar in the fuel tank? A wire loosened?"

"Nah, not that I know about anyway."

"Extra ten for an honest answer."

"Hey, I been tellin the truth!"

"You see anyone get on my boat while I was gone?"

"No!"

"You get on my boat while I was gone?"

I watched him squirm a bit and glance up.

"I just petted the kitty. She seemed lonely and was crying up a storm so I opened the door and reached in and petted her. But that's all. I didn't go inside. I swear!"

"And no one else did either?"

"Nope and I was kinda keeping an eye on your boat."

"Waiting for the goons to arrive?"

He at least had the conscience to blush. "I didn't know that was who was coming."

"But you had an idea."

He nodded glumly.

"Okay, hopefully no harm done. Here's the twenty bucks."

"I can't take that!"

"Why not? We had a deal? Did you tell the truth?" He nodded. "Well then, the twenty's yours."

"Yeah, but I sicced those guys on you."

"That you did. But you also told me what I needed to know, so, a deal's a deal." I handed him the two tens and he reluctantly stuffed them in his pocket. "Let me know what I owe for the fuel. Give me a shout out, I'll be up top."

He nodded, glad to be left alone. And I wanted to have a moment to think.

Chapter Thirty

I laid back on a lounger and looked at the sky. It wasn't about me. The kid had been paid to call if the boat showed up. I didn't think the former Mrs. Stan had this kind of pull, but I wasn't positive. I jumped up, hopped over the rail and landed on the back deck. "I'll be right back!" I called to the kid who was still fueling. I ran up the dock to a souvenir shop I had seen on my way back to the dock. I ran in and grabbed a postcard of Pamlico Beach. "Do you sell stamps here?" I asked the woman behind the counter as I gave her the nickel for the card.

"We do and you can even drop it in the mailbox right outside."

"Perfect."

I gave her the stamp money as well.

"Got a pen I can borrow? I guess I didn't come very prepared."

She laughed and handed me the pen she had tucked behind her ear. "Me, I always have a pen."

I wrote the coffee shop's address and thought for a minute about what to say.

Lou Anne. Everything going great. Weather has been good and boat is running fine. Hope you are well. Coffee pot is always on here! Tell Stan I met some friends of the boat's. Lots of questions. Big guys, seemed wise. I said little and they left. Feeling lucky if you know what I mean! Headed south. Hellos to Ned. Hugs to you, Lou Anne.

xox

I licked the stamp and handed the pen back to the woman. "Thanks for the loan." She smiled and waved. I dropped the card in the mailbox just outside the door and headed back to the dock. It was time to get out of here

.

Chapter Thirty-One

I paid for the fuel and waited for the lines to drop away, kicked the engines in gear and pushed out into the channel with a small salute to the kid on the dock. I hoped he had told the truth about no one doing anything funny to the boat. Once I was a mile or so down the way I tucked into a cove, and dropped the anchor.

"Okay, missy, we are going over this boat top to bottom to be sure everything is as it should be. And why were you crying loud enough to get that kid on board petting you? Jeez. Where is your pride?" I gave her head a ruffle as I headed below. She followed me as I worked my way up from the bilges. All the wires looked snug and no tools were out of place. The engine room was its usual clean and orderly. I checked the oil and the transmission fluid to be sure they hadn't been drained or fouled. The propeller shafts looked seated and the collar around them was dripping just the right amount. The Raycor was clear so no water in the fuel. All the hoses were clamped down tight. No unusual leaks. I checked all the portholes below deck to be sure they were secure and not open to the sea. The V-berth was neat and tidy like I had left it when I cleaned yesterday. My cabin had its usual amount of disarray but nothing unusual. The intake on the head was shut off properly, no inflowing water. I opened my closet and pushed the shoes aside. It didn't look like the floor had been disturbed but I still needed to know for sure that the money was still there. I used my knife blade to lift the door on the hidey-hole. Still lots of money laying in neat stacks, undisturbed. I fitted the floor in place and shoved the shoes back on top of it.

The salon and galley were exactly as I had left them. The main deck head was also shut down as it should be. I went back up top and checked the captain's cabin. I crawled under the desk and repeated the process of pulling up the floor, to check on the contents of the second hidey-hole. Money still there and looked to be untouched. The helm station was last. Bosco followed me in and hopped up to her bed. Everything looked to be as I'd left it, until I looked more closely at the drawers. The bottom one was not pushed all the way in. I tried hard to remember if I might have left it ajar. It was possible but not likely. "Did you open this drawer? Did you stick your little paw in here and pull real hard?" A brief halt in the bath to give me a fleeting glance. "Yeah, I didn't think so." Nothing seemed disturbed in the drawer, it just wasn't shut right. I checked the second drawer and it was the same. Seemingly undisturbed. I pulled the top drawer open and looked for the envelope of money. Not where I remember putting it. It was gone. So maybe the dock kid had come up looking for cash. Not an unusual thing for a boat to have. Or someone else had come looking for drawers full of money and been disappointed. I was hoping it was just the dock kid, but I had a feeling it wasn't. I wondered if I had seen the last of Frank and his boys.

"Okay, Bosco, we have a couple of choices. We can keep heading south to Alf. We can turn around and go back, or we can sell the boat and head for the hills. You got a preference?"

A soft mew was my answer. "Yeah, I don't see where turning around will help. I'd just be driving right back to where I started and probably more wiseguys. Selling the boat means finding a new life again. You may have nine but I'm not sure I do. I don't want to start over and I don't want to walk around the country with a sack of money on my back. So I guess we just keep going south to meet up with Alf. But when we do, I think I may have to tell him about Frank and his buddies just in case they cause trouble for me. At least someone will know where to start looking for me. I don't think I will tell him about all the money, not at first anyway. You, little one, are the only other living thing that knows about it. Well, you and whoever put it there in the first place. Can't forget them. 'Cuz I have a feeling they haven't forgotten the *Mist B Haven*."

I went forward and pulled the anchor and then steered us back out into the channel headed south. I was pretty sure the boat hadn't been tinkered with but I sure had been.

Chapter Thirty-Two

The rest of my trip to Savannah was relatively uneventful. I contacted Alf by radio and let him know when I was within two days of arriving, so I knew which marina he was using and found him waving me into a slip right next to his. I backed the Mist B Haven into the narrow space and Alf tied off the stern lines while I hopped forward and tied the bow lines to the posts sunk on the port and starboard sides. Then I raced aft to receive a big bear hug from my friend. It was so good to see a familiar face!

"Pulled her in like an old hand, Girl. Well done!"

"Had a good teacher." My smile was so big it was hurting my face. "I am so glad to see you Alf."

"I'm glad to see you, too! But I gotta tell you I wasn't sure you would come."

"Why?"

"Oh, I don't know. Guess I thought you had better things to do than follow some old geezer around. And Lou Anne had said you were looking pretty settled in, so I just figured you would stay put."

"Well, I probably would have if you hadn't sent word. I wasn't sure where to go or what to do. And I knew my way around Jersey City. But Alf, it gets cold up there!"

"Yes, it sure does! Glad you got out before the ice and snow set in. Once that happens it gets hard to move."

"Well, no one ever showed me where the heater was on this boat, so it was either come south or freeze! Hey, why are we standing out here like a couple of strangers? Come on in, let's have a coffee or a beer if you'd rather."

"Beer sounds good. You got any cold in that old icebox of yours?"

"Ah, come see for yourself!" I led the way inside and forward to the galley. "Ta da!" I gestured with a flourish towards the new refrigerator. I pulled two very cold beers out of it, used the bottle opener on the end of the counter to pop the tops and handed one to Alf.

"Well, here's to an excellent improvement!" He smiled and touched the neck of his bottle to mine.

"I'll drink to that!" We both smiled and sipped.

"Where did you get it?"

"Billy set me up with the Handlys. They gave me a pretty good deal, I think, and installed it, too."

"Nice."

"Yeah, it means I don't have to stop for ice every two days and deal with a bunch of water sloshing around the floor as it melts. Plus, veggies and fresh meat." I opened the door to display my stock.

"Nice. You get a grill set up yet?"

"A grill?"

"Yeah, I'll show you mine. You mount it off one of your rails over the side so it doesn't set your boat on fire. You can grill a burger or steak lickety-split. Throw a salad together and you have a fast meal at the end of the day. You should think about it."

"I will. Maybe I should bring a couple steaks over and you can give me a demonstration."

"Now you're talking!"

Just as we were getting ready to step back out onto the deck, I heard a thud as Bosco hopped down through the galley cabinet from the helm station. Alf's head whipped around towards the sound. "You got someone else on board?" he asked in a slightly hurt voice.

"Well, kinda." I went back into the galley and scooped her up. "Alf this is Bosco, Bosco this is my friend, Alf." She turned her green eyes at him and mewed softly.

Alf laughed. "Friendly?" he asked as he reached out a hand to scratch her head.

"Far as I know she is, but you are the first person I've introduced her to. So we'll have to see."

I set her down and she began to wind herself in and out of Alf's legs.

"Friendly, I'd say," he chuckled. "Okay, get yourself settled in. Guy at the dock office is expecting you. I paid for one night to hold the slip for you. Bring your steaks and a couple beers around sunset. I'll fire up the grill and we can eat and catch up."

"Sounds great. I'll see you in a couple hours."

Chapter Thirty-Three

I liked that he hadn't crowded me by staying for a long visit. I needed time to settle in, as he put it, and get my boat secured and the slip paid for. Just get my legs under me. I was glad to see Alf. But I was glad when he left, too. I wondered if that was weird. And decided not to worry about it.

I went up to the helm to get some money from a newly restocked envelope, then headed down the dock to find the office and check in. I took one of the local maps they had on the counter showing where the grocery, marine supply store and package store were. All the essentials for a boatie, I thought to myself. I noticed a trading library as well. So I could bring my read books and exchange them for new ones. Well, new to me. None of these books were new. But clearly other people read a lot, too. This was a busy marina with a lot of boats coming and going. I paid for the slip for a week to ensure that I would have a place to stay. Then I wandered up to the main street and spent an hour window shopping and getting the lay of the land a bit. This marina was on the outskirts of Savannah, but I could see that it was an interesting place and that I would enjoy a few days here to walk in the old part of town and soak in some of its history. I had been so focused on not missing Alf that I hadn't done any sightseeing on my way down. This seemed to be a good location to start. I assumed Alf was probably ready to move on but even if he was, I could stay on and see things and catch up with him again later. I could imagine us dropping into a rhythm of time alone and then meeting up again for a few days. Who knew what was in front of us?

Chapter Thirty-Four

As I headed back towards the boat I began to think about whether to tell Alf about the money I had found and the visit from the wiseguys. I was torn about talking about the money. On the one hand it might feel better if someone else knew about it. But it also meant that in some ways I was less safe. The more people who knew about it, the more likely the original owner would show up wanting it, if he hadn't already. It also increased the risk of someone boarding the boat and robbing me. Not that I thought Alf was going to rob me or blab about the money, but like the war slogan said, 'loose lips sink ships' and I knew the best way to keep a secret was to not tell it to people.

I arrived back at the dock still unsure of what to do. I changed into a clean tee shirt and jeans. Grabbed the steaks and beer and went next door to Alf's. I would decide if the moment presented itself. Alf's boat was smaller than mine by a good fifteen feet. It had a smaller salon and the V-berth was the only cabin below. But it was snug and he had it all well-organized. He was out on the back deck when I arrived, heating coals on his grill, which was, as advertised, hanging off the starboard side rail held by two clamps.

"Permission to come aboard?" It seemed so formal, but Alf had explained that it was like knocking on someone's door rather than just walking into their house. Boats were more public. We often are sitting outside which made it all the more important to respect each other's space and ask before intruding.

"Yep, especially since you are bringing dinner!"

I slid over the stern gunwale of the *Swede Sea* and handed him the steaks. "Want a beer now?"

"Nah, I'll wait till dinner, but feel free."

"How 'bout I leave two here and put the rest inside to keep cool?"

"Excellent. Bring the salad when you come, will you?"

When I came back outside, the smell of the cooking steaks was overpowering. "Whoa, how do you keep everyone from trying to join you for dinner? Those smell great!"

"Yeah, they do. I usually don't start grilling till late, so everyone else has already had their dinner!"

"Clever. So show me how you rigged this thing up. It does look very handy and I am tired of pan frying everything!" He showed me how it clamped on and the modifications he had made to the grill itself to allow the clamps to work. It seemed like a workable system and I was eager to install one on my boat.

"This is very cool. Would you be willing to help me set one up?"

"Absolutely. That's why I invited you to dinner, so you could see it in action, and also because I saw those nice steaks in your fridge! You like yours rare?"

"Sure, why waste time burning it to shoe leather?"

He pulled the steaks off the grill and handed me the plate, "Here's the best part. When you are done you just release this lever and you can dump the hot coals overboard. So bye bye fire hazard." The coals let out a loud sizzle when they hit the water and then they were gone.

"Let's eat up top. Serve yourself some salad and bring your beer. The sun is about to set, so put a move on!"

Alf had built a cozy banquette like seating area under the windows of the helm station and we slid in opposite one another with our plates and drinks.

"So tell me about your trip down, Girl. How'd it go?"

"I'm too hungry to talk. You go first."

He laughed, but then he did. "Well, I hit weather right off the bat and got caught out in the open with some pretty big seas, but that only lasted a day or two and then I could sneak back inland to the waterway and that provided some protection. I threw a propeller two days out of here. Had to climb in the cold, dark water and mount my backup. Must have caught a bug and the flu whacked me a day later. So I was happy to put in here. Other than that it was a pretty uneventful trip." He laughed at how that sounded and so did I.

"I stopped a lot along the way and caught up with some old friends who were heading south as well. There are a bunch of us 'snowbirds' who go north for the summer and south for the winter. I have been doing it long enough that I know a good number of the boats and people. Made it fun. It can get a little lonely cruising all by yourself after a while. I guess you might have noticed that."

"Yep, I did." I leaned back away from my empty plate and smiled. "The book idea really helped, I gotta tell you, that and Bosco. I like having another living thing on board with me."

"I can understand that. Though it can be hard to keep animals safe on boats."

"Yeah, I thought about it, but I think if I keep her inside she will be okay. So far she doesn't seem too interested in coming out on deck, even when I am out there. I guess I will have to wait and see how it goes."

"So what made you think of getting a cat?"

I told him the story of the drowned mother cat and kittens.

"Yeah, I've heard that folks do that sometimes. Get over populated and instead of finding them homes they just chuck them in the water. I guess it would be the same at the rescue shelter, but at least they get a shot at getting adopted before they kill them. So, you got the lone survivor?"

"I did. She was just a bit of a thing then. She is growing like the proverbial weed right now. Sometimes I watch her sleeping and I swear I can see her legs getting longer!" We both laughed at that.

"So if I get us another beer, will you tell me how your trip went?"

"I will but just bring me a glass of water, will you?"

"Water!?"

"Yeah, cold water. If you have any."

"No problem"

He disappeared below taking the plates with him. I sat looking out at the last of the twilight and wondered once again how much I should tell Alf. I realized how very little I really knew about him. I knew him as a man who was willing to help a young single woman learn how to run, repair, and care for her own boat without expecting to be paid in cash or "favors". I had never felt any sexual tension between us. He had never been anything but kind to me. But what if he knew there was a couple million dollars hidden in the floor. Would he still be my kind friend or would he decide I should pay him for services or would he be a thief? I didn't think it would change how he was with me, but I wasn't sure. I didn't want it to change anything...but...

"One water." I jumped, startled. "Hey, where were you? Deep in some kind of thought, huh?"

"I guess so, though I'm not sure I could tell you what that thought was."

"Well, tell me about your trip?"

"It was actually pretty fun. I was glad to have a destination. Thanks for inviting me to join you. I'm not sure I would have known where to go if you hadn't."

He smiled and nodded. "I figured."

"I didn't hit any really bad weather. That storm that came up kept me inland through the Chesapeake instead of going out into the open ocean for that leg. So that worked out. I didn't do any sightseeing, I didn't want to risk missing you and I wasn't sure how long it would take me to get here. I realized after a week or so that every day was different and yet also the same."

"How do you mean?" he interrupted.

"Well, all the same in that I am out on the water motoring along every day, doing the same routine, coffee, breakfast, get underway, lunch, drop anchor, dinner, read, sleep, do it again."

"And different?"

"Even though I was motoring every day, some days I got farther than others, some days I used more fuel than others, some days there was a lot of other boat traffic, or none. Just subtle differences that made each day different from the last. I liked it. I kept a log and could compare fuel consumption, wind and seas, currents. By the time I got here, I have begun to have a sense of how far I can go on a gallon of fuel given different conditions. Every day offered a chance to learn something new, to add to the stock of data and experience I have. It's kinda cool."

"Yes, it is. And the longer you do it, the more you know and the more you know you don't know. If that makes any sense."

I nodded and we both laughed. "Yeah, it makes sense. I am pretty clear after just this short cruise that I know almost nothing, but I know way more than when I started."

"Exactly." He sipped his beer. "So did you stay in marinas or find other people to go parts of the way with?"

"No, I usually dropped anchor in a protected bay or cove. Sometimes I rented a mooring from one of the marinas, but I didn't like staying tied up to land anywhere overnight. I think it might be different for you."

"Why?"

"Because you're a guy. Everywhere I pulled in to get fuel I got stared at, and that was the easy day. Usually there were comments and guys wanted to hitch rides, or asked to come aboard and look around, when clearly they were asking to come aboard with no intention of leaving. It felt like if I stayed tied up at the dock overnight, I wouldn't be safe."

"Wow. I guess I hadn't thought of that. I always find interesting people when I dock overnight. That's why I do it."

"Well, I met some interesting people all right, but I didn't like it that much."

"But you seemed okay in Jersey City."

"I was, but mostly that was because of you. Folks saw me with you and they left me alone. And after you left the guys at the dock were so used to me, I was like a little sister by then.

They felt like it was their place to look out for me in a big brother way. If I was off the dock I didn't go that far away and people knew me. Lou Anne threatened a guy with a pot of hot coffee just before I left."

"Really?"

"Yeah, he was in the coffee shop and I was looking at my charts and he decided he should come with me. And when I politely declined his offer he called me a dyke and it went downhill from there. Lou Anne stepped in and offered him the choice of hot coffee down his front or being on his way."

"Wow."

"Folks looked out for me because they knew me. But once I left that dock there were no big brothers to watch out for me. There was just me. I scared off a couple guys with my gaff. In fact, someone told me I should get a shotgun to use instead of a gaff."

"Hmm. Are you thinking about it? Sounds like that might not be a bad idea."

"Oh, Alf, I have no idea where I would find a shotgun, let alone how to use one! I'm a city girl, not some country squirrel-hunter."

"Well, hunting squirrels is very hard, I'll tell you. You want to start with a bigger target and work up to squirrels."

"Okay, that was stupid to say, but you get my point. I don't know anything about guns."

"You didn't know anything about boats either but it didn't stop you walking onto that one and acting like you intended to stay." He nodded his head towards the *Mist B Haven*. "If you want to get a gun I will help you. I do know how they work and I can teach you. It might make you feel safer, I don't know."

"Well, I don't know either but it can't hurt to see, I guess. But only if you have the time before you head out again. I don't want to hold you up. And if I have to choose between the gun and the grill, well, those steaks were awfully good, and maybe I could just throw the hot coals at whoever oversteps himself."

"No need to choose. I got no schedule but to be near Jost by New Year's Eve. So we have some time, don't worry."

"What's a Jost? Not to change the subject!"

"Jost Van Dyke. It's a small island in the BVI."

"BVI? Isn't that some kind of underwear?"

"That's BVD's." The eye roll that went with that made me laugh.

"Oh, right. I knew that. I just wanted you to say it! So what is the BVI?"

"The British Virgin Islands. Southeast of Puerto Rico. Jost is one of the smaller islands and it's kind of a tradition for a few of us to gather there for New Year's Eve. We smoke and drink and eat lobster and shoot off fireworks and have a great time. Every year it gets a little bigger. Friends invite friends. It's a chance for me to catch up with old friends and make some new ones. I look forward to being there with that gang. I need to leave here with time to get there. So we have a week. How's that?"

"A week is good. Hopefully I will be able to return the favor and invite you to a grilled dinner sometime soon on my boat!"

"That's the goal, Girl. And to set you up so you can shoot your dinner if you want to."

I laughed and got up. "Thanks for the dinner, Alf. I'm really happy to see you but I gotta head home. I'm a little tired and I want to check on Bosco. She tends to tear things up if I leave her alone too long."

"Yep. I'm happy to see you, too, Girl. Come have coffee in the morning and we'll figure out the day."

"Deal." I patted him on the shoulder as I went by. "Sleep good."

"You too. And holler if you need anything."

"Will do."

Chapter Thirty-Five

All seemed quiet on the *Mist B Haven*. I found Bosco curled up on my bed with only a couple books on the floor. Maybe tomorrow I would sort through the ones I wanted to keep and those I wanted to trade in for new ones. Restock not just the food supplies, but the food for thought supplies, too!

I climbed into bed careful not to disturb the sleeping kitten, soon to be cat, and turned out the light. Sleep was not coming anytime soon. My mind was still on what, if anything, to tell Alf about the money hidden away on the *Mist B Haven*. He never asked me how I supported myself or the boat, where the money for fuel and supplies came from. I never asked him either. I just assumed he was retired. But I was nowhere near retirement age. Maybe he thinks I am a rich divorcee, or a trust fund baby. I could keep on just not saying anything but it seemed weird. There would be purchases to be made tomorrow for the grill and the shotgun if I decided to get one. I would just pull cash out of my pocket and that would be that. But he had to wonder. And what kind of friend was I not to trust him? But it didn't seem that easy. Maybe I could tell him about the drawer money and not the major stash. The probable mob money. Lucky Luciano's money. Would I put him in danger if he knew about it? I hadn't thought I was in any real danger till Frank, Carlo and the crew showed up and it still wasn't clear who they were and what they wanted. But it had to do with the boat and I could be pretty sure that the original owner of that couple million dollars probably wanted it back. Why bring another person into that problem? It was my problem, not Alf's.

My mind mulled it over but eventually sleep overtook me. The sound of kitten purrs in my ear woke me up about the same time as the sun. It was too early to go to Alf's. I made coffee, went up to the helm station and restocked my pants pocket with cash. I stood sipping my coffee looking out at the gray morning light and thought my life was more odd than I could have imagined. Standing on the deck of my very own boat, stocked with millions of dollars that didn't belong to me, and yet, who else did it belong to? Was I just some banker, holding their money till they were ready to come get it? Perhaps I should see myself as a trustee of the money. Deciding how and when to spend it for the actual owners. Currently I seemed to be spending it on me! I wasn't even keeping track of how much I "owed" the drawer any more. I was just keeping a log of expenses as if it were the boat's money. Which, in a way, was the real truth. It was *Mist B Haven's* money. It was all hers.

"Hey, are you having coffee already?"

"I am, but I will happily drink yours. Somehow you seem to have the better coffee pot."

"Well, bring your cup and come on over."

I climbed down to my main deck and jumped from my boat across to Alf's.

"Girl, I would be careful doing that. Someday you'll lose your footing and end up in the drink. And that will get you a reputation and a good laugh from everyone in the marina. To say nothing of falling into some pretty disgusting water. This is not your local swimming hole, you know. You and your young legs that you think won't fail you."

"Yep, that's right, my young legs and I are pretty sure we can jump four feet. So relax, old man. I am not going to fall in the drink."

"Ah, pride goeth before a fall you know. And who are you calling old?"

"Well, you are older than me, for sure! So that makes it a true enough statement."

Alf snorted, "Hell, eighty percent of the population is older than you are! Your *boat* is older than you!"

"Aw, hush up and let me get some coffee. It is too early for your yip yip."

We both laughed and I scooted into the galley to refill my cup. Back up on the top deck we sat exactly where we had sat last night and looked the other direction at the still low hanging sun.

"Looks like it might be a nice day. Let's set your grill up and go out and see if we can catch something to put on it. What do you say?"

"I say what time does the shop open and should we load any of your rods on my boat while we are waiting?!"

And that is what we did for the two hours that we had to wait for the hardware store to open. We picked out a couple of Alf's deep sea fishing rods with big reels and heavy line and carried them to the back deck of my boat and fitted up some pipes on the rails that would work as rod holders.

"Didn't you do any fishing on your way down here?"

"I did but I wasn't out in the open ocean that much and I only have spin tackle on board. I would cast off the stern after I anchored for the night and hope for some poor unsuspecting blind fish to bump into my hook. You would be surprised at how many fish I caught with pieces of hot dog!"

"Hot dogs? Really"

I nodded. "Ugly, stupid fish, but good pan fryers."

"Maybe we should buy you a deep sea rig so you can catch a real dinner. Marlin or sailfish."

"You can't eat those. Even I know that." I interrupted.

"Sure you can, but really, why would you? Those are fish that are so fun to catch you get them to the boat, take a picture and let them go."

"If I have to work that hard, I want to eat it in the end, so I would be hoping for tuna."

"A good choice, but you wait till you hook your first billfish and fight it all the way in. You might change your mind."

"If you say so. How much would it cost to get me set up?"

"Well, there's the rub. That rod you just put in that holder with the reel and line would run you three or four hundred dollars. Deep sea fishing isn't spin casting."

"Apparently not. But maybe we should see what kind of deal we can find for me. Seems like it would be a good piece of equipment to have on board."

"Let me check around and see if anyone is selling anything. You might be able to pick up something decent for a couple hundred."

"That sounds like a good way to go, but I will have to rely on your judgment since I know nothing about fishing really."

"I kinda guessed that when you said you were using hot dogs for bait!"

"Hey, it worked!"

"Come on, let's go see if the hardware is open, I can't take much more of this!"

I laughed, knowing he was teasing me. "Fine. Let's go buy things!"

"Okay!"

Chapter Thirty-Six

It didn't take as long as I thought it would to purchase and install the grill. It looked complicated but it was really a fairly simple arrangement. We installed two clamps that held the grill to the rail. A single rod ran through the clamps and when pulled, the clamps loosened enough to allow the grill to be tipped overboard, emptying the coals.

"Just remember your dinner goes with it! So try throwing a bucket of water at it first. Puts out the fire and salts your food at the same time."

"Got it. And I am going to keep a full bucket handy while I have the grill going. Fire scares me."

"Me, too, especially on a boat. This thing could burn to the waterline in minutes and that's barring the propane tank exploding first."

"Okay, that's not a happy picture. How about we go fishing?"

"Excellent. You fire her up and I'll drop the lines."

"You got it. Drop the bowlines first will you?"

"Aye aye, Captain."

Once we were out in open water and far enough from shore not to worry about running aground, I put the boat in neutral and went down for my first lesson in deep sea fishing, how to bait a hook with something other than a hot dog. Once we had a ballyhoo on each hook, Alf sent me back to the helm to re-engage the engines.

"Let her run as slow as she can," he shouted up from below as he paid out line and locked the reels down. "You keep a real heavy drag on the line so that when a fish hits it, it will really sing out and hopefully he won't empty your reel before you can get below to start reeling it back in. Okay, hold her steady now."

Alf ran up and stood at the helm. "I'll take her. You go outside and watch the lines. If something hits one, let me know."

"Why, what do you do then?"

"You throw it into neutral until you can start reeling the fish in and then the helmsman tries to help the fisherman by not letting the fish get under the boat or too far away."

After an hour of running with only a couple nibbles and nothing staying on the line I was getting bored. "Hey, how about some hot dogs?"

"Yeah, we aren't having much luck. Fire up the grill and toss a couple on for me, will ya?"

I laughed. "I was thinking for bait, but lunch sounds fine, too."

"You are not putting hot dogs on the end of any line of mine, Girl."

"All the more reason to get one of my own. Then we can have a fish-off and settle this once and for all!"

"Deal."

We eventually cranked the lines in so they wouldn't foul the props when we shut the engines down to eat. We sat on the loungers on the upper deck and ate the hot dogs I had grilled up along with potato chips and some coleslaw I threw together.

"Good eats, Girl. Thanks."

He set his empty plate on the deck and lay back. "Boy, these loungers were a great find! They are perfect for a nap!"

"Yes, they are, and I got a deal on them, they were free! Someone had set them near the trash at the dock so I dragged them home. They are pretty excellent. And free is a good price. I'm always watching what folks throw away. It is one way to stretch a dollar and some folks don't have enough sense to know what something is worth."

"Or maybe they don't care. They figure they are done with it and maybe someone else can use them."

"Right, but why not sell them instead of leaving them in the trash?"

"Too much trouble? I don't know. Any way you look at it, you were the lucky recipient though."

"Yeah, and so were you." I gave his leg a slap as I leaned over to pick up our plates. "Have a nap. I'm going to clean up the galley and feed Bosco and maybe drop a hot dog overboard to get us some dinner for later."

"Ha ha ha."

By the time I had finished cleaning up, it was time to head in if I wanted to navigate the channel while it was still light. I fired up the engines. Alf sat up on one elbow, but I waved him back down. "Relax, I got this. You go back to sleep." He gave a feeble wave of his hand and lay back down. It made me happy to be motoring towards shore with a friend and a cat sleeping soundly. They had confidence that I could keep them safe while they slept. I liked that. Being a real captain, responsible for all souls on board.

Chapter Thirty-Seven

The next morning was pretty much a carbon copy of the one before, only this time we drank our coffee and waited for the gun shop to open.

"So, what kind of gun do you want?"

"I don't know. I'm not even sure I want one. It just seemed like an interesting idea and possibly a smart thing to have around."

"I think that might be right. I have one."

"You do?!" I was stunned. "You never told me that."

"I hate to break it to you, but there's a lot I don't tell you!"

"I know, sorry. I was just surprised, that's all."

"Why?"

"Well, I guess you never struck me as a man who would have a gun."

"And what kind of man strikes you as having a gun?"

"Someone with harder edges. With a deader look in their eye than I have seen in yours."

"You are so full of baloney!" He laughed. "You have no idea what you are talking about. A lot of people have guns, for a lot of different reasons. Sport, protection, hobby, history. There are a bunch more but I will stop there. Not everyone with a gun has a dead look in their eyes and murder on their brain, for goodness' sake. Hell, you don't and you are going out to get a gun. Do you think some dead look will come into your eyes when you purchase it? That you'll be changed forever?"

"No."

"So why should I not be a man who owns a gun. Because I seem normal to you?"

"Okay, okay. I get it. Sometimes I say stupid things."

"Yes, you sure do! Good thing I like you." He smiled and gave me a friendly pat on the back. "Come on, let's go buy you a dead look!"

"Very funny. I'm not going to hear the end of that, am I."

"Nope, probably not!"

By the time we had walked up the dock and found the shop, we had settled on a pump-action shotgun for me. Alf suggested that it was a good choice for self-protection and scaring people away. "Just the sound of the shell being racked is enough to send most sane people ducking for cover. Plus, a shotgun doesn't have to be carefully aimed. Point it in the general direction and pull the trigger, it sends out a broadcast blast of shot. Doesn't do as much damage as a single bullet, but it will give a person pause."

"The scare them off is appealing to me. I don't really want to seriously hurt anyone; I just want to keep folks away from me when they have other ideas."

"Yep, I think this will be the ticket."

We tried out different makes and models and finally found one that had a short barrel, an easy pump action and a weight that seemed comfortable for me. We bought it and two boxes of twenty gauge shells for $250. The shop owner tossed in a sling to carry it over my shoulder with. I didn't bother to explain that I wasn't going to carry it anywhere. It would hang on my boat. I just said thanks. He wrapped everything in brown paper and Alf and I picked the parcels up and carried them back to the *Mist B Haven*.

"Okay, let's figure out how and where you want this mounted, then we can take it out on the *Swede Sea* and practice using it. What do you say?"

"Good with me. I think I want it where I can reach it easily and yet where it isn't obvious. Like mounted under the gunwale near the cabin end of the back deck."

"Okay, port or starboard side?"

"Port, I think. Right below the grill. That will help hide it and it's an easy place to get to quickly."

"Got it."

It wasn't long before we had fashioned three hooks that the gun rested in. The sling turned out to be helpful in that it could be tightened down to snug the gun up against the bottom of the gunwale but a hard pull and the whole thing was in my hand. It would take practice to get it to be a smooth fast move, but I could see how it would work and was willing to perfect the movements.

"This is perfect, Alf. No one can see it and yet it is easily accessible."

"Yep. The low visibility is important. You may end up going places that don't want you bringing in a gun. You tell them you have it and they will either confiscate it or not let you enter their waters. This way you just don't declare it and no one is the wiser. If anyone finds it you smack your head and say you totally forgot it was there. Or better yet, claim you didn't know it was there."

"Where can't I take a gun?"

"Tons of the island nations don't allow them. The BVI, for a start."

"So what do you do about your gun?"

"Same as you're going to, I hide it and lie." He gave me a sly smile. "You got to let your pirate out a little sometimes. Now grab the gun and ammo and let's fire up my boat and go practice."

"Where are we going?"

"Out where no one can hear or care what we are doing. And maybe where the fish are running so we can eat tuna tonight!"

"Excellent! Give me five minutes to close everything up and I will be over."

Chapter Thirty-Eight

"I am really glad we didn't bring my boat," I said as I raised the shotgun from a resting position in front of me to my shoulder and fired. "Bosco would probably hate this."

"Yeah, loud noises like guns and fireworks can really get animals going. Sometimes on New Year's when we start shooting off the fireworks you can hear some of the island dogs howling over the noise of the fireworks! It is pretty impressive. You should think about coming down to Jost for the party. I could introduce you to a lot of folks and you can quit being such a loner."

"I am not a loner."

"Okay, you are not a loner, but I seem to be the only friend you have. What do you call it?"

"Picky."

"Okay, well come to Jost and quit being so picky!"

"I will think about it, Alf. I will, but right now I kind of want to do some sightseeing and rest for a week or so. I am just not ready to motor on yet."

"Well, that's okay. It will take me almost twice as long to get there as it will you. I only have one screw to your two."

It still sounded odd and almost dirty to call the props screws but that is what they were. They screwed themselves into the water with each rotation. Still I was more comfortable calling them props.

"Right, but I am not sure I am ready to run in the open water for extended periods. Heck, I can't stay awake for days on end like you do, I gotta get my beauty rest."

"And you think I don't?" He asked sweeping his graying hair back dramatically.

"Well, how do you steer or stay on course while you sleep? You can't be anchoring out there and floating around without power isn't a good option, even I know that. So how do you sleep and run at the same time?"

"Autopilot."

"Autopilot?"

"Yeah, autopilot. I attach it to the wheel, set my course and it holds to that while I sleep. Now mind you I sleep pretty lightly and I wake up a lot to check on it, and I sleep right up by the helm. That's what those bunks are for! I don't sleep great, but I sleep."

"Huh."

"Didn't you use your autopilot on the way here?"

"No. I don't think I have one."

"Oh man. I am so sorry. Yes, you do. I should have showed you how to use it."

"Are you sure I have one?"

"I'm not positive, maybe Stan's wife took it, though why she would is beyond me, but I am pretty sure you have one. Stan used it all the time. So there was a rig set up at one time and I am pretty sure I remember seeing it. I just didn't think to show you how it worked! But as soon as we get back we can check and I will teach you how to set it up before I leave. So if you want you can motor down to meet me and not be so sleep deprived you start hallucinating before you even get there."

"Gosh, that would be great! I kept wondering how I would ever go anywhere very far off shore without crew. Now I know, you get fake crew!"

"That's it exactly. Single handers have been doing it for a long time. I don't like having someone else on my boat. Oh, every now and then I get a hitchhiker wanting to come along from one place to another. Like the little bastard whose clothes you inherited. But mostly, I enjoy running alone and if I want to move long distances, the autopilot is the only way to do it. Of course you need to be careful about staying out of the shipping lanes because it just steers to your set course. It doesn't see. The danger is getting run over and sinking."

"Now there's a pleasant thought." I positioned the shotgun and fired.

"Yes, but if you pay attention to the charts and don't go near the lanes when you are on autopilot you are pretty set. Of course there is always the possibility of running into another boat on autopilot but the chances are slim of that happening."

"Unless you are like the most unlucky person in the world, in which case I would guess it's a sure bet that you will!"

"So are you saying you are the unlucky person? Cause I gotta tell you, you sure don't look like it to me!"

"No, I know I am not the most unlucky person. In fact, I think I might be the opposite. I was just meaning that even when you think the chances of something happening are slim, it doesn't mean it won't still happen."

"I suppose you are right, Miss Merry Sunshine. But I will still use the autopilot and I bet you will, too."

I nodded, "Yep, I probably will, but if I sink out there, know I went down shouting 'I told you so, Alf!'"

"I will remember that for sure," he chuckled. "Here, try to hit this." He threw an orange in the air and waited.

Chapter Thirty-Nine

It turned out I did indeed have an autopilot rig. It was in a chart drawer. I had seen it when I initially went through the boat but I had no idea what it was and left it where it lay. Alf quickly set it up and showed me how to set my compass heading and engage the device. Once it was set up it was a pretty simple process.

"This is very cool!"

"Yep, it is. I wish I had the patent on it, I would be a rich man."

"You seem like you are doing okay."

"Oh, I totally am, I am just a little jealous of how simple and perfect this is and somebody else invented it!"

"Could you have invented it?"

"I don't know. Maybe. It is beautiful in its simplicity. I am a more complicated kind of guy. I like thinking up more convoluted stuff."

"So you really are an inventor, you weren't just kidding around?"

"I am a type of inventor but I don't talk about it much."

"Like it might jinx your ideas if you tell someone?"

"Sort of, yes, that is a good way to put it."

"Okay, I won't ask you anymore. But I *am* curious. So any time you feel like bouncing ideas around...."

"You'll be the first place I will bring the ball." He smiled and stepped back from the machine. "Okay, see if you can dismantle it and then reinstall it by yourself."

"Easy-peasy." And it was. "I feel pretty confident I'll be able to do this by myself. Thanks for showing me this, Alf."

"You are very welcome. It may take some adjusting as you learn your boat and how it steers with the autopilot engaged. But I'm sure you will get the hang of it. Now nothing should keep you off the bounding main!"

"Whatever that is."

"Right, whatever that is."

We laughed easily. "I think it might be beer and sunset time. I'll be right back with a couple cold ones if you want to stay a bit longer."

"Always willing to have a beer. Bring them on!"

I dropped over the rail, a short cut to the galley and returned with two icy beers.

"Here's to having an extra hand on board without having to have it be a person!"

"I'll drink to that!"

We laid back on the loungers and watched the sun disappear over the water.

"How well did you know Stan, Alf?"

"Not very. I mean, he was around the marina a good bit over the years and I would see him on the *Mist B Haven*. Why?"

"I have just been thinking about him a lot lately. Wondering what his deal was or is."

"Well, he was always friendly, offered a drink when he saw me, didn't ask a bunch of nosy questions, and was willing to lend a hand if I needed it. That about sums up my definition of someone I am happy to have around. Don't really need to know a bunch more. Knowing someone's work history or birthplace doesn't tell me much about them. How they act to me and to others, that's what is important to me. And Stan always acted like an upright kind of guy."

"Yeah, he did, didn't he."

We sat silently. Alf waited to see if I wanted to take the conversation any further. I decided to deal with him exactly like he described. He had always been friendly to me, offered me a drink when he saw me, didn't ask any nosy questions and was more than willing to offer a hand when I needed it. I had never seen him do something that I thought was unkind and he had always treated me respectfully and generously. What did I want? A resume with references? I was the reference. I either trusted myself and my judgment or I didn't and if I didn't whose was I going to trust? I took a deep breath.

"Did you know he gave me this boat?"

"No, though I suspected it was something like that. When his wife or whatever climbed aboard and took everything that wasn't nailed down off her, I figured it was a matter of time before he wanted no part of her, the boat. I knew he already wanted no part of the wife."

"There was a bunch of money on the boat." I said it so quietly I wasn't sure if he had heard me. I waited, not really wanting to repeat myself.

"What do you mean there was a bunch of money on the boat?"

"Just that. The former Mrs. Stan took just about everything, you were right. Remember you gave me a blanket because I had nothing. But apparently she either never went into the captain's cabin or someone put it there after she left.

When I finally started cleaning I opened the three shallow drawers in the cabinet in there and they were stuffed with money, paper money. A lot of paper money. Big bills, too!"

I stopped myself. I realized I was starting to babble and my voice sounded borderline hysterical to me. I felt like a dam whose flood gates had been opened, but I needed to close them again, quickly or I was going to tell him about the second find and I really wasn't prepared to do that yet. One step at a time.

"So how much are we talking here?"

"Somewhere around $170,000."

He let out a low whistle. "Wow!"

"Yeah, wow."

"Did you ask Stan about it?"

This was the one question I was dreading because I didn't like my answer. "No."

"Why not?"

"I don't know." He waited, watching me. "Okay, I was afraid of his answer. I was afraid he would take it all back and I wouldn't have it. I don't have any money of my own and I would be broke. Or that he was some kind of criminal and the money wasn't his either and I would lose it. I wanted it to be not his and yet his. Like he was giving me the boat and a way to support it. And if I asked about it he would reconsider."

"So mostly you didn't want to lose the money that wasn't yours to begin with. Is that right?"

"I know it sounds terrible,"

"Is that right?" he interrupted.

"Yes, I didn't want to lose the money because--"

"Ah, ah, ah, no because. There is no follow-up excuse. Did you think about Stan in all of this?"

"What?"

"Stan, did you think about him? Maybe he needs this money. Or maybe it isn't his and someone will come asking him for it and he doesn't have it. Maybe it's his wife's and she comes looking for it and it's gone and she goes after Stan, or worse, sends someone else after Stan. Money, big money like that doesn't get stuffed in a drawer and forgotten. You need to figure out whose money you have been spending and how to get it back to them. Grow up, Girl. This is real life, and no amount of magical thinking is going to make it anything but real life. You think some fairy godmother waved a wand and a hundred and seventy grand just shows up? No. That money belongs to somebody and it isn't you."

He got up, set his bottle on the floor and disappeared down the ladder.

Chapter Forty

I lay there staring up at the sky. At first I was furious. "How dare he?" But that quickly turned to "How dare he what?" He had said nothing that I hadn't at some level said to myself. It wasn't my money, no matter how much I wanted it to be. It wasn't. And there might be consequences for it not being where it should be, with whoever it should be with. I was running away because I didn't want to lose something that wasn't even mine, but that I had liked thinking of as mine. I was a thief. That thought stopped me in my tracks. I was a thief and Alf knew it. That was why he had walked away. Because I was suddenly not someone he wanted to know. And that was when I started to cry.

I wasn't crying big tears like when Alf had left the first time. These were just water coming out of my eyes and running down my cheeks and neck, soaking the top of my tee shirt. A tee shirt Alf had given me when he didn't know me at all except to look out and see a lost soul standing forlornly on the dock in a dress and ruined heels. I had been so out of place it must have been hard not to laugh. He had shown me how to be in this world of boats and water. He had clothed and fed and sheltered me. And now he knew I was a thief and a fraud. How would I ever make it right again between us. I wasn't sure, but I was sure that I wanted to try. Disappointing Alf was bigger than anything else I had done and I didn't want to keep doing it. I wanted to be the person he saw only two months ago, the spunky young woman he had been proud to know.

I lay out on deck looking up at the stars. Hoping for answers or a plan. Neither came. Just before I finally drifted off to sleep his words came back to me, 'Grow up, Girl.' and that is what I intended to do. Though I only had a glimmer of an idea of how to try.

Chapter Forty-One

I woke up early with a fine coat of dew soaking my clothes, giving me a serious chill. I went below to my cabin and fired up the shower. Standing under hot water always helps me get some perspective and it warms me clear through. I got out and put on an old pair of khakis and a clean tee shirt. Bosco had been circling my legs and crying since I stood up. She almost followed me into the shower to keep up her racket. I knew she was hungry and wouldn't leave me alone until I fed her. So I went up to the galley, started a pot of coffee and put some kibbles in a dish for her. Peace restored, I took my mug of coffee back up top into the helm station. I picked a chart and began plotting a course across the open water, writing potential autopilot headings on the white margins of the map.

I heard Alf moving around his boat and I went down to the main deck and out onto the dock. I stood at the stern of the *Swede Sea*, screwed up my courage and called out softly. "Permission to come aboard?" and I waited. I could hear him but no answer came. I knew I should walk away, that he was telling me he didn't want to see me. But I couldn't quite do it. "Alf, I know you are awake and I know you don't want to talk to me, but I would appreciate it if you would listen. Just for a minute."

The main cabin door opened and he leaned against the jam with his arms crossed and a blank expression. This was my only chance to try to make it right. I didn't want to screw it up, I hoped I wouldn't and that it wasn't too late.

"You were wrong, Alf." His eyes narrowed and I saw his weight start to shift away from the door frame he was leaning on.

"I did think about Stan and what might happen. I just didn't care enough about anyone but me to do anything about it. I was wrapped up in what I wanted, what I thought I needed and let that veto any thoughts or concerns I had for anyone else. I was selfish in a very childish way. I didn't care what happened to other people as long as I got what I wanted. I know at the moment I look like a thief to you. I do to myself, too. And I know I have disappointed you and betrayed our bond. So here is my plan. I am going to head back north tomorrow or the day after at the latest. I'm going to a place where I think I can contact the people who are interested in the money. And I will figure out who it belongs to and I will return it. And make an arrangement to repay what I have spent. I am going to get a job once I get back north and stick with it until I can pay back every cent that I took that wasn't mine. I am going to contact Stan through Lou Anne and see if there is anything I can do for him to make it right that I drove off with a ton of money that wasn't mine. I am going to try to grow up, like you suggested. I am sorry I didn't do it before. And that it seems to have cost me your friendship. I will treasure everything you taught me and hope I can make you proud to know me again. Thanks for listening, Alf. I appreciate you taking the time." I turned and headed back to the *Mist B Haven* feeling both heavier and lighter. I needed to start stocking my boat for an ocean voyage back to Pamlico and the tattle-tale dock boy.

"That's a good start, Girl." His voice was so soft I wasn't sure I had heard it. I turned to look back at him. "Any boat set on autopilot will stray off course slightly. The longer it stays on autopilot without any attention or correction, the farther off course it goes. You have been running your life on autopilot and haven't been checking your direction. I think you strayed a bit. Now you are choosing a direction and setting a course for it. It's a start at growing up."

I nodded, not knowing what else to do and not wanting to ruin the moment. I turned back to my boat and climbed aboard. I went into the galley to start a list of supplies I would need. Since I would now be paying for them I scaled back the "wants" and stuck to the "needs". More canned goods, less fresh or expensive meats and vegetables. Beans and rice would become a staple in my life and luxury items were just that, a luxury I couldn't afford.

I went topside, pulled out my red wagon and headed up the dock to the grocery to start crossing things off my list. I tried not to look at Alf's boat as I passed. I knew I needed to start doing things on my own again and I needed to pay attention, like Alf had said. Quit letting my life run on someone else's chart or no chart at all.

Chapter Forty-Two

I stopped by the post office and bought a couple stamps on my way home from the grocery. I also ducked into the dock store and picked out a pretty postcard of downtown Savannah. It showed a house with a long drive and trees covered with Spanish moss. I pulled my full wagon towards my boat and noticed the slip next to mine was empty. Alf was gone. I wasn't really surprised. But it made me feel even more alone than I already did. But there was some relief there, too. I wouldn't have to try to avoid him nor he me. It felt like we had said all that we were going to say and now it was about me doing something or not.

I unloaded the supplies onto the deck and then started carrying them into the galley to stow them. Bosco followed me back and forth across the salon, stopping at the door, unwilling to venture out onto the deck. "Well, at least you aren't deserting me." She turned her green eyes towards me. "Okay, I haven't been deserted exactly. Maybe I should say my actions have caused someone I admire to move away from me. Is that better?" She wound herself between my feet. "Yeah, I am starting to get that what I do has consequences. I need to notice that and choose my actions more wisely. To quit making excuses for myself. But I have done pretty good by you, Bosco. I have managed to keep you fed and safe. Maybe that is how I start changing. Notice what I am doing and whether it reflects how I want to be or not. Time will tell."

I carried the last load in and secured the galley drawers and doors so any rocking motion wouldn't turn my supplies into lethal projectiles hurtling across the cabin. I went below to my cabin to gather up all the dirty clothes and linens. I grabbed a notebook and walked back down the dock to the laundromat.

I stuffed two washers with laundry and soap and sat out in the sun to wait while they churned around getting clean. Clean clothes, clean start. I could hope. I pulled out a pen and the postcard I had chosen earlier, propped the notebook on my knees and began to write.

Hey Lou Anne.

I know you prefer pretty, so how's this beautiful house in old Savannah? I haven't had much time to sight-see. Alf and I have been busy updating systems on my boat. We installed a grill so I can cook hot dogs and remember you! He left this morning. I am heading out tomorrow. Will try to send more postcards. I think of you often and send warm smiles and a wave.

I set the postcard aside and got up to check the washers. They had hit the final spin. I waited for them to finish and loaded two dryers before heading back outside again. The sun felt good and I leaned back against the warm wood of the building and once again propped the notebook on my knees. This one would be harder to write.

November 4, 1960

Stan.

I am hoping that Lou Anne was able to deliver this fairly quickly after she got it. I am in Savannah for another day and then will be heading back north to Pamlico Beach and possibly back to Jersey City if I need to.

I don't know if you know about this or not, but I am guessing you might. I found a bunch of money ($176,110.00 to be exact) stuffed in the three drawers in the captain's cabin on the Mist B Haven. I found it before I left Jersey City. I found it before you signed the title over to me. But I didn't ask you about it or mention it to you. I kept quiet because I wanted the money for myself.

I didn't have a lot of financial resources when you met me. In fact, I had the money in my purse and that was it. So I saw it as a way for me to keep moving forward.

I reread the last paragraph and drew a heavy line through it. I heard Alf in my head, no buts, no excuses. Grow up. I had begun to understand that meant take responsibility for myself and my actions.

I apologize for that. It was a selfish thing to do. I understand that it is not my money, though I have been acting like it is. I am not sure if it is your money or your ex-wife's or whose. That doesn't really involve me. I just know it isn't mine.

I am heading back to Pamlico Beach because I believe there may be some men there who have an interest in it. I met several of them when I was docked there a couple weeks ago. I mentioned it in a postcard I sent to Lou Anne, though I was a bit cryptic about it.

I am not sure if they were interested in me and the Mist B Haven because of the money or if they were representing your ex-wife. She was coming down the dock with several guys in suits the morning I was leaving Jersey City. Billy recognized her and suggested I pull off before she reached us. It seemed like good advice at the time. Now I am not so sure. I motored away from her because I was afraid she would take the boat from me. Again, I was focused on what I wanted and not concerning myself with much else.

I don't really know what the Pamlico Beach crowd wanted. They just asked a bunch of questions about who owned the boat and for how long. They wanted to board her, but I managed to avoid that and was able to motor away without further incident.

I do know that one of the marina workers had been paid to call and notify them that the Mist B Haven was at the dock. So someone was clearly looking for her for some reason. I am going there to see if I can find out who they are and what that reason might be.

Stan, I am sorry if my leaving with this money has caused you any trouble. I want you to know I am on my way to try to make it right. I have used about two thousand dollars to make repairs and to stock and fuel the boat. I intend to get a job so I can pay it all back as soon as I can. I realize I should have asked you about the money as soon as I found it. It was childish of me to think it would magically become mine if I just pretended it was.

I intend to make this right, Stan.

I will be at the Pamlico Beach marina in a week. Please write me with instructions. I will do whatever you suggest. If I don't hear from you I will continue on to Jersey City and try speak to you in person.

Please contact me if you can.

I reread the letter. It wasn't perfect, but I hoped it was a start at repairing the damage I might have done. I slipped it into an envelope and sealed it. I wrote on the front 'Lou Anne, will you please try to get this to Stan as quickly as possible? Thanks!' Then I addressed another envelope to Lou Anne at the coffee shop. I put the postcard and the letter to Stan in it, sealed it up, put stamps on the front, walked up to the post office and dropped it in the mail slot. No turning back now.

Chapter Forty-Three

My laundry was dry and I gathered it up and went back to my boat. A sailboat was in the slip next to me. Alf really was gone. I gave the new neighbor a nod but kept going, not wanting to engage in conversation at the moment.

I went below and stowed the clean clothes and remade the bed. I picked up the stack of books I was going to trade at the book exchange, rifled the pages of each one to be sure I hadn't left anything in them and took them topside to take with me on my next trip up the dock. I set them on the stern gunwale and went back inside to get my wallet. I needed to go settle up with the dock master, pick up one more chart and check the latest weather report so I would be ready to pull out early in the morning.

When I came back out, my new neighbor was squatting on the dock looking at the titles of the books I had left out.

"Are you getting rid of these?"

"I was going to take them up to the dock office. There's a book exchange there."

"Well, I know Charlie would love a couple of these. And I see several that I would enjoy, too. How about if I go get some of ours and we swap before you take them up to the exchange? Might save us both a trip."

"Fine by me. I can wait a few minutes."

"Great. I'll be back in a flash." She hopped up and quickly disappeared down into the cockpit. I took the chance to study her boat. Sailboats are so different from motor vessels. They seem to have less room, partly because they need to be more aerodynamic or whatever the water term is for sleek. So they are generally narrower and also lower to the water. No second deck for a sailor! I could see the appeal in a way. Wind is free. No big fuel bills certainly sounded good right now. But with free came a loss of speed. Sailing often requires tacking back and forth so the boat's sails can fill and push you forward. There is rarely a straight course heading for a sailor. With a motor vessel I can point my nose where I want to head, fire up the engines and go. Plus, I can go pretty much whenever I feel like it. A sailing boat needs to wait for wind. No doldrums for me! This one was a good looking boat, deep blue hull and a beautiful teak deck. According to the lettering on her hull she was home based in Bermuda and her name was *Sister C's*.

Who thinks up these names, I wondered, not for the first time. It was as if every boat had to have some clever, or not so clever, pun or word play or double meaning in the name. Starting with my own. The *Mist B Haven*. I wanted to rename her but everyone I talked to said it was bad luck. I agreed it was bad luck, I owned a boat named *Mist B Haven* and I couldn't change her name! That was some kind of bad luck indeed. One of my current boat naming theories is that boaties have so much time on their hands they spend part of it dreaming up stupid names for their boats to kill some of it. Maybe I would check it out with the folks aboard the *Sister C's*.

My new neighbor's head popped back up from inside the sailboat and she came out carrying a nice stack of books. A second head appeared. "Come on, Charlie, don't be shy. If you want new books, you best get up here or I will have first dibs on everything. I am not picking out books for you this time. All you did was whine about what I chose last time. Come on, get out here." She looked at me and rolled her eyes. "Very sweet, but very shy."

"I heard that." The other woman muttered, climbing slowly up onto the deck.

The first woman handed me her stack of books, "See what you think." I glanced quickly at the titles and saw several I would happily read.

"Yep, I think we got ourselves a horse trade! Come aboard and we can do some swapping. Would you like a beer or coffee?"

"Nah, we won't stay that long, but thanks for the offer. Maybe another time."

"Maybe, but I hope to head out tomorrow morning."

The second woman, the one called Charlie apparently, was standing on the dock by the stern of my boat. "You can look through the books up there if you'd rather, but it might be easier and more comfortable sitting down here instead of squatting up there."

She stepped over the rail and down onto the deck. "Squatting anywhere gets tiresome for me."

I looked up and realized she was probably right. She was the tallest woman I had ever seen.

"Six three and a skosh," she said. I must have looked confused. "That's how tall I am, six three and a skosh. It's usually the first question folks ask."

"Oh. I was going to ask if you wanted something to drink."

She started laughing. It was a big laugh and quite contagious. Pretty soon all three of us were laughing and wiping tears from our eyes. "Well, if you put it that way," she managed to choke out, "I reckon I could use a beer!"

"Two." Her friend held up a finger.

"Couple beers coming up." I ducked inside still chuckling. Grabbed three bottles, popped the tops and went back out to my guests. They had regained a measure of control as had I and we all just sort of smiled and shook our heads. "Well, here's to first impressions," I offered and clinked bottle necks.

"Ouch," Charlie said. "Not sure that's a good thing." though she was smiling when she said it.

"Sure, it is." I replied. "Having a good laugh right off the bat can't be bad, especially for the sweet but shy types."

She glanced at me to see if I was making fun of her. "I was referring to myself, though I am not really sure about the sweet part."

She relaxed and smiled. "Me either. I'll let you know." That made us both chuckle again.

"Well, let's get down to some book trading."

We all sat on the padded bench on the back deck and looked through each other's books. There were plenty to swap. I replenished my library in short order with Perry Masons and other 'who dun its' from Charlie and a selection of higher-brow fiction from Clara, as she had introduced herself. They seemed to be equally happy with many of my books.

"I'd say this worked out quite nicely. I have a much smaller stack to carry up the dock, that's for sure!"

"So, you said you are heading out tomorrow?"

"Yep, I hope to."

"Where are you heading?"

These are pretty standard questions to ask in a marina, but I wasn't sure how much I wanted to tell strangers, no matter how much we seemed to hit it off. "I'm going north for a while."

"Wow. You know it's getting on winter up there, right?" Clara gave me a concerned look.

"Yeah, I know, but I got business up there so not a lot of choice. I am hoping to get up there quick, get stuff taken care of and be back down in the warm as soon as possible." I knew that part wasn't probably going to happen. I would have to get a job and earn $2000 and that would mean staying up north for at least six months. But I wasn't about to tell these women my full plan.

"How about you two? Are you planning on staying here or heading off again?"

"We hope to restock here and then head farther south. We like being in the BVI for New Year's."

"Huh, I have a friend who likes to do that, too. I was thinking of going that direction but then business came up and now I am headed in the opposite direction."

"Who is your friend who travels in the BVI? Maybe we know him."

"Or her," Charlie added in a soft voice.

"Right, or her."

"Alf Lidstrom."

"We know Alf!" they said in tandem. "He has the *Swede Sea,*" Clara added.

"Yep, that would be Alf."

"We usually see him somewhere along the Intracoastal and then for sure we meet up with him on Jost for New Year's."

"What is it about New Year's on Jost that is so special? Alf got kind of glassy-eyed about it, too."

They both laughed. "Well, I guess you will just have to come down and see for yourself some year, won't you?"

"Even shy girls like us can have a good time there," Charlie added.

"Huh. So how do you know Alf?"

They exchanged glances and Clara, the talker of the two, piped up. "Well, if you sail or motor on the Intracoastal for very many years, you begin to see the same boats and you end up in the same marinas so you strike up conversations, kinda like this. You find kindred souls, people you connect with for one reason or another, and you make plans to meet up occasionally. That is part of what New Year's on Jost is. It's a chance to catch up with other boating friends at least once a year. How do you know Alf?"

"We were both in a marina up in Jersey City and he gave me a hand working on my boat. Actually I was new to all this and he taught me how to run the boat as well as repair it. I owe him a lot."

"Hmmm, that sounds like Alf. He always has time to offer a hand or a drink or if nothing else, a smile. He's a good one, that Alf."

"Yes, he seems to be."

"Well, we should be going. I'm sure you have a ton of things to get done if you are going to get underway tomorrow." They each gathered up their books, set their empty bottles on the table and shook my hand. "It was nice meeting you."

"It was nice meeting you too, Clara. Please tell Alf 'hey' for me when you see him, will you?"

"I sure will."

"Maybe you ought to come say 'hey' to him yourself." Charlie had hold of my hand.

"Maybe I will sometime."

"Well, it was nice to meet another shy girl. Come meet up with us at Jost. It would be fun."

"I'll keep it in mind."

"You do that, sweet one, you do that." She gave my hand another squeeze and clambered over the stern rail and on to her own boat. She gave a wave and disappeared down below.

Chapter Forty-Four

I took my new books inside and down to my cabin to secure them on the shelves. It felt good to have new things to read. I was surprised, but it had felt good to visit with Charlie and Clara, the C's of the boat name. I doubted they were actual sisters. Clara might have hit 4' 10" if she was wearing shoes. That disparity alone was a pretty good indication of no shared gene pool. They did have a connection that ran deeper than friends it felt to me. There was a familiarity and an affection I didn't usually pick up between friends. I didn't really care. They were the first women I had seen that weren't attached to a man. I hadn't even seen a lot of couples out on the water. As I got farther south, I had been seeing more. I was at the tail end of the snowbirds heading south, so maybe I wasn't seeing as many as I would have had I been a month earlier. It still seemed like a man's world out on the water, so I was glad to have met a couple women. It felt like company to me.

Once I had the books secured, I went up the dock with the leftovers and found a couple more at the exchange I was happy to add to my collection. I paid off my dock fees and bought the new chart I wanted. The latest weather report was posted on the bulletin board outside the office door. I scanned it and wasn't happy with what I saw. An early winter storm was brewing out in the Atlantic. It didn't look like it would come in close to shore, but it was the weather. No one really knew.

I was planning on covering the distance from Savannah to Pamlico Beach mostly in the open ocean. The Intracoastal was much more protected, but it would take me three times as long. Now that I had an autopilot, I could run out in the open water and catch some sleep while the boat steered itself. But I wasn't looking to be out in open water if a storm came up. I knew I wasn't seasoned enough to handle big waves and high winds. I decided to plan my course as though I was going to be in the open sea and check the weather again before I left in the morning. If it looked iffy, I would stay close to shore and duck inland if it looked to be getting bad. The problem with that plan was, once I got to the Carolinas, the barrier islands were just that, a barrier. There were only a few places that had channels deep enough to run through and get shelter. Time would tell. I already had a course plotted for the inland route since I had just come that way. I would just need to work backwards.

I took my new chart and a copy of the weather back to the *Mist B Haven* and went into the galley to grab a sandwich before I started plotting the new ocean route. Bosco was her usual hungry self. I filled her bowl with new kibbles and gave her fresh water. "Growing kitty still needs lots of food, right?" Her purring seemed to answer in the affirmative. She busied herself with the kibble and I munched away on the ham and cheese sandwich I had put together. I decided to put on a pot of water to boil for rice. If I was going the open water route it probably wouldn't be calm enough to have a pot of boiling water on the stove. I leaned against the galley counter and waited for the water to boil. Once it did, I put the rice in, set a timer and went into the salon to wait. I had left one of my new books out on the table so I stretched out on the couch and began to read. Bosco, happy with her full belly, hopped up and padded around my stomach until she found a comfy spot and curled into a purring ball. I awoke to the timer ringing and a punch in the belly from a startled cat.

"Thank goodness for timers, eh, Bosco? I know it startled you but I could have burned the rice, the pot and the boat if I had slept too long! Better a little startle now than a big smoke-filled startle later." I took the pot off the fire and turned the burner off. A couple of stirs with the fork and the rice was fluffy and perfectly done. I would let it cool, then put it in a bowl to spoon out under canned beans for meals while under way. Hearty, easy-to-make food. That was the ticket.

With the rice cooling and the stove turned off, I finally headed up to the helm to do my plotting. I spread the chart on the table and got lost in figuring out course headings and currents. It was like a puzzle figuring out where to go and what would influence each decision. I referred to the weather report for projected wave heights and direction. It was an absorbing task and I hardly noticed time going by.

Chapter Forty-Five

"Halloo the *Mist B Haven*." The call surprised me, I was so lost in plotting. I stuck my head out the helm door and saw Clara standing on her boat looking up at me. "I couldn't help noticing your grill, I have a couple steaks I would be happy to share and do all the cooking. What do you say? Wanna have dinner with us?"

I hadn't noticed how late it had gotten or how hungry I was, and I really had no reason to say no. A steak cooked by someone else sounded great, too.

"Okay, that actually sounds great! The charcoal is in the portside stern gunwale locker. I think I have some vegetables or maybe salad fixings."

"Nope, we have it all covered. But how about you play hostess and we eat on your boat? Ours is a bit cramped for three."

"Well, that sounds like a great offer. Hard to refuse. Thanks."

"Good. Figure on eating in forty-five minutes provided you like your steak rare."

"Oh, yeah. Just so it doesn't walk off my plate!"

"You got it. Hey, don't forget to stow your fishing rig. I lost an excellent rod that way. Forgot I had it on deck, sailed out of the harbor into waves and that was the end of that rod. I saw the grip as it slid across the deck and disappeared overboard. Very frustrating."

I had no idea what she was talking about but she went back below before I could ask her. I shrugged and turned to head back to finish the charting. I looked out over the bow and then I understood what she was talking about. Sitting across one of the loungers was a deep sea fishing rod and reel set-up. I went out to look at it. There was a note tied to the reel. I was torn whether to read it, but in the end curiosity won out over caution. I untied it, opened it and read.

Thought this might come in handy if you are heading back through open water, which I assume you are. Fresh-caught dinner has a real boosting effect when all you can see is water.

You were wrong, too. I am still your friend. I will always be your friend. But that doesn't mean I will always like you or approve of your choices. It means I will help you when I can, if you ask, and that I wish the best for you always.

Go do the thing that will make you proud of yourself, Girl. That is the most important thing. To be able to look at yourself in the mirror and not be ashamed. I want that for you. I want it very much.

You have everything you need to succeed. Chart a course and stay true to it. Wear your life jacket, tether up when you are in the open water, stay out of the shipping lanes when you sleep and keep your radio on one six.

I look forward to meeting you again, to see who you choose to become.

Sail safe.

Alf.

This time I didn't cry. I held that piece of paper to my heart and smiled. I hadn't lost Alf. At least not totally, not yet. But I knew if I didn't go set things right, I wouldn't be the person I hoped to be or that he hoped I'd be. I needed to do exactly as he said. Set a course and stay true to it. I had begun; I needed to finish. The fact that somewhere Alf was waiting for me to show up and be that person gave me a sense that I was not alone, like I had felt this morning when his slip was empty.

I picked up the rod and taped to the handle was a smaller note. "No hot dogs allowed," I laughed. Alf was still with me. That felt good.

I stuck his notes on the wall of the helm station and went below to stow the rod and be sure everything was straightened up for my visitors. Dinner sure smelled good!

Chapter Forty-Six

It turned out Charlie was in charge of the grill and Clara had put out quite a spread on the table in the salon.

"You are just in time to show me how to get rid of the coals," the tall woman said.

"Pull the rod under the clamps and they will tilt overboard." I explained.

"Ah, very slick."

"Yep. Alf set it up for me just this week."

"So like him. We were sorry he was gone when we got here. We are running a bit late and I guess he went on."

"He left this morning."

"Well, we will catch up to him soon enough, I have no doubt. Come on, let's eat!"

We sat at the table and passed dishes of baked potatoes, corn, what looked like homemade biscuits and, of course, the steaks around the table. It got quiet as we all dug in and enjoyed the meal.

I pushed back from the table a bit. "Man, you two eat like this all the time?"

"Oh no! Clara likes to cook and bake, but it's hard to do while we are underway. When we hit port, we usually go big for a few days to make up for the cold sandwiches and canned goods we have been eating."

"It's a little way of celebrating being tied up. I love being out on the water, but I like to make a proper meal, too. We were glad you were willing to join us."

"I just made a big pot of rice and was going to start eating it with beans tonight. You saved me from that fate! And I sure do appreciate it. Coffee for anyone?"

"Coffee would be perfect. I hope you saved room for pie."

"Pie?"

Charlie laughed. "Oh, C thinks it isn't a real dinner if you don't have dessert. She baked a cherry pie."

"Wow! Well, I didn't save room but I will make room, that's for sure!" I cleared the plates off the table and took them into the galley. Clara had brought more than just the food, she had brought plates and flatware as well. I realized I had bought only one place setting, figuring it was always going to be just me on the boat. Once again, I saw the selfishness in my decisions. When I returned to the salon there was a good-sized piece of pie and what looked like whipped cream at each place.

"Holy smokes! This looks great!"

"Wait till you taste it." Charlie warned.

I smoothed the cream across the top of the pie and took a bite. "Heaven, pure heaven."

"Oh I am so glad you like it." Clara smiled proudly.

"Ever have anyone not?"

Charlie snorted, "Not likely!"

"Well, now you can never tell. Some folks like cake more than pie."

"Not if they taste like this, babe."

Clara shot Charlie a dark look and Charlie looked uncomfortable and fell silent.

We each ate looking down at our own plates for a few moments. I wasn't sure how to reestablish the friendly warmth that had disappeared like a wisp of smoke. But I knew I wanted it back. I thought about Alf and how he would handle it. "OK, something just happened that turned this place into a deep freeze. I'm not exactly sure what it was, but I would bet it wasn't the pie. Did I do something that bothered you?"

"Nah, it wasn't you. Clara's mad at me. We probably should be going." The big woman started edging her way out of her chair.

"I'm not mad. It's just sometimes I wish you were more careful about what you say."

Charlie stopped getting up and looked at Clara. "What, like you think this young one hasn't caught on yet? You really think we are that invisible? Look at us. Look at me! Do you really think people don't get it? We don't look like sisters; I don't care how much you think some stupid boat name will make folks believe we are. Sometimes I just get tired of pretending I don't love you. So I slipped and called you 'babe' in front of a new friend. So what? It's like Popeye says, 'I yam what I yam.' I am proud of you, of how smart and pretty and talented you are. Why do I have to pretend I'm not? Who does it help? You? Me? Her?" She reached across the table and took Clara's hand gently in hers. "You are the best thing that has ever happened to me, babe. Sometimes I just get tired of people not knowing that."

I could see Clara's eyes filling.

"Oh," I said. "Okay, good to know. So I shouldn't call either of you 'babe' in public, right?"

Both of the women turned to me with puzzled looks on their faces, then they saw my smile.

"Right. No babe in public if you want to keep the peace," Charlie said, starting to chuckle.

Clara nodded, laughing a bit herself.

"Okay, any rules on 'sweetheart' or 'honey'?"

That was all it took to push them over the edge, we were all roaring with laughter and calling out other possibilities.

"Snookums?"

"Honey-bunny?"

"Love bug?"

Eventually we ran dry and the laughter quieted. "Whew! If I had known I was going to laugh that hard I might have eaten less. I feel kind of sick! Just kidding. I might have waited on the pie though! But it sure was good, babe," I added.

Clara looked at me for a moment, smiled and said, "Well I am so glad you enjoyed it, babe."

"Hey, who are you calling 'babe', babe?" Charlie interrupted with mock jealousy. That sent us all into another fit of laughter. We eventually settled down and worked together to clean up the dishes and table. "We really should be going. If you are leaving in the morning you need to get some sleep. There won't be much good sleep once you get underway until you get back inland."

"Yeah, I am a little nervous about that. I figure it will take me six days to get up past the barrier islands to the mouth of the Chesapeake. I will pull in there and rest for a couple days, I hope."

"Just watch the weather." Charlie cautioned. "If it looks like it will get bad you scoot yourself inland as quick as you can. Even a good-size yacht like yours is better off out of big seas."

"Will do."

We trooped out to the stern deck and stepped over the rail onto the dock. "Thanks for making dinner and inviting me. I really enjoyed myself. I hope we see each other again."

"Oh, I think we will. You know where we are every New Year's," Clara reminded me. "You take care and sail safe."

"I will try."

She gave me a hug and started tugging Charlie down the dock. "Calm seas, young'un" she called over her shoulder.

I watched as they climbed onto the *Sister C's* and waved.

"Good night, babe," I called quietly.

"Good night, babe." They replied in unison and then disappeared below.

This must be what Alf was talking about when he said he met good people along the way. I could imagine sailing around by myself if there were friends I could see occasionally. This could be a good life if I could figure out a way to support it, other than using other people's money.

Chapter Forty-Seven

The next morning, I was up early. I was eager to be underway as soon as it was light enough to get off the dock and see my way to the channel markers. I went up to the dock store for one last weather report. It wasn't terrible, but it wasn't great either. The storm in the Atlantic was moving very slowly towards shore and was predicted to make landfall south of Cape Cod. That would keep it north of me, but seas would be rough from the backwash. There was nothing to do but start and see what happened. I had listened to enough talk around marinas to know that there was never a perfect time to head out into open water. There were just better and worse times. This was somewhere in the middle. I would go.

I took a copy of the teletype report and walked back to the *Mist B Haven*. Charlie was standing on the dock waiting for me. "Hey."

"Hey, yourself." We smiled at one another. "I found this under the cover flap of one of your hardbound books. Wasn't sure if it was yours or someone else's, but it isn't mine. I thought maybe you should have it back." She held out a thin packet of folded papers.

"Thanks." I took them and shoved them in my back pocket.

"You ready to go?"

"I think I am, ready as I'll ever be."

"Scared?"

"A little."

"Good, that means you have an idea about how big a thing you are doing. Never underestimate the ocean. She's beautiful but she will make arrogance and ignorance pay. Trust me."

I nodded.

"You'll be fine, young one. Pay attention and when in doubt, trust your gut." She gave me a pat on the shoulder and stepped back, "You need help dropping lines?"

I nodded again. "That would be great, thanks. Can you give me five minutes to get ready?"

"Take your time. I have nowhere to be and I have a coffee sitting on deck. I'll be ready when you fire up those big engines of yours."

"Great."

I went below for one last check to be sure everything was secured. I checked the bilge pump to be sure it was working and the connections were all snugged down. I hooked the V-berth door open so it wouldn't bang around once we were underway. I did the same to my cabin door and made sure the salon doors were latched closed. I filled a thermos with coffee and stowed the pot. "Okay Bosco, we are ready to go, I think." I climbed up to the helm and started the engines. True to her word, Charlie appeared at my stern waiting for directions.

"Stern lines, then bow. Leave the breast line for last. I might pivot off it."

"Aye aye, Cap. Hey, where's your jacket?"

"Huh?"

"Your life vest? Why aren't you wearing it?"

"I have it up here. I don't wear it though."

"Well, you should. You are going out into the open ocean. At least wear a floater so they can find you if you fall overboard."

"I'm not going overboard. I stand in this cabin and steer. It isn't like a sailboat where you are walking around the deck."

"Suit yourself. But remember what I said about ignorance and arrogance."

"God, you and Alf. Okay, okay, I am putting on my jacket. Does that make you happy?"

"Yep, it actually does. I want to see you again someday, young one. Leave it on after I'm out of sight too, will ya?"

"Yeah, I will." I smiled at how she had figured right. I intended to shed the bulky life vest as soon as I was in the channel.

"Stern is free." She called in a quiet voice but one that carried enough for me to hear her. "Bow is free."

I watched her settle midship with the line loosened but still snug against the dock post.

"Let me know when you are ready."

"OK, let her go," I called and pushed the port throttle just enough to pivot around the pilings and out into the channel. "Thanks, Charlie!" I gave a wave as we straightened out and began to slowly move away from the dock.

"Sail safe, babe," she called. "Sail safe."

Bosco came and sat on the ledge under the windscreen and looked out. "OK, cat, here we go. Northward ho!" I steered us out the main channel, through the cut and into the waves of the open ocean. "We are going to take these pretty much right in the nose for a while and then I can turn us and set a more comfortable course." She turned her head and watched me as if she understood. "Here's hoping you don't get seasick!" I laughed only half joking. "You might want to get in your bed and lie down for this part." Again the head turn, this time with a look that could only be called disdain. "Okay, fine. Sit right there, but don't blame me if you fall off."

We bucked out into the waves for another thirty minutes, then I turned and quartered them, set the course I had written in the chart margin and began to relax. I realized I had been standing the whole time and I slid back to sit on the stool that was bolted to the floor right behind me. Bosco seemed to understand that the scarier part was over for now and she curled up in her bed and dozed. I hadn't realized she was standing watch with me until she wasn't. I smiled. It was good to have company in the adventure, even if it was only a cat.

As I settled in to hold course, I felt the packet of papers I had forgotten. I pulled them out of my pocket, unfolded them and flattened them out. The paper and tiny handwriting were the same as the sheet I had found when Bosco had torn every book off the shelf. The "money can't buy good fortune" guy. I looked out over my bow making sure I had a clear path and was holding to the compass heading I had chosen. I thought about how I had a different take on that phrase than the last time I had considered it. Maybe he was right after all. The money I had, that I had thought of as mine, wasn't. It hadn't brought the good fortune, I thought, but the loss of respect from someone I admired and from myself as well. It had possibly cost the man who had given me the boat, I wasn't even sure how much. It had become a burden. Maybe that was what the guy was saying. Money didn't buy the good stuff, it just bought stuff.

I checked my position one more time and then settled back to read the pages.

Chapter Forty-Eight

August 20, 1953

600 hours

I wish I had never taken this job. I can't really write a proper log, never have been able to. The guy who owns the boat wouldn't allow it. Now I know why. I thought I was working for some company that owned this yacht, turns out I am working for the fucking mob! I should have known it was too sweet a deal to be legal. But I ignored all the warning signs because I wanted the damn money. Greed, that's how I end up out here floating around with a boat full of drugs and cash and a mob boss who is supposed to be in exile in Italy.

I wrote a quick one paragraph last night as the storm was picking up. I stashed it in the book I was reading, but I can't find it right now. I want to write this all down so there is a record of what happened. If I make it through this, I am jumping off this boat as soon as I get it docked and I am never looking back.

We started this trip as a fun fishing trip for four corporate guys, at least that was how it was presented to me. I brought them out to fish and they start telling me to head to Cuba, and oh, by the way, we need to rendezvous with a boat and pick up another passenger. I wasn't happy but they were paying my salary and so I set up for Cuba and radioed our position to some boat and they show up with the new guy. I didn't recognize him right away, but eventually I got a good look and I realized I had Lucky Luciano on board. We pulled into Havana and everyone gets off. I am told to refuel and wait, they won't be on land long and I need to be ready to pull off when they get back. So I fuel and wait.

It must have been a couple hours later, here comes Lucky down the dock, just him and another guy I have never seen. They are each carrying a suitcase. They step on board and sit in the salon. If I stand on the back upper deck I can hear pretty good what they are saying. I am curious and figure it won't hurt. I hear them talking about some guy, Genovese. They seem to be arranging a hit on the guy. I wished I had stayed in my cabin, but now I'm afraid to move for fear they will hear me and that will be that. The new guy is telling Luciano that the money is his and that only the two of them know about the deal and the money.

"It would cost us both dearly if the other families realize we have made a pact to join up and start a war that weakens them," the new guy says.

"I understand," Luciano replies. "I don't really want this money, I have no way of returning to Italy with it and I do not want anyone to know of our arrangement. I feel it best to take it so you are as tied to this as I am. And so that it costs you something as well as costing me."

"I understand," the other guy says.

I can tell this meeting is drawing to an end, so I crouch down behind the railing and wait while the visitor leaves the boat and walks down the dock. I hear Luciano dragging the suitcases down below to his cabin. He comes back topside half an hour later with the two suitcases. Only this time he isn't dragging them. They seem to be empty or at least much lighter. He walks to the end of the pier and tosses them into the

*water Then he turns and walks back down the dock and
out of the marina.*

*I can't help myself. I go down below and look around
his cabin. I can see nothing out of place and no sign of
what was in the suitcases. I didn't spend a lot of time
looking through drawers or anything, but there was
nothing in plain sight, that was for sure.*

*I went back topside and waited some more. Another
couple hours, here comes one of the "fishermen" and a
guy pushing a cart with a bunch of banana boxes. He
tells me to help him load them into the V-berth down
below. There must have been twenty boxes and they
were heavy. We crammed them onto the berths and
floor and they pretty much filled the room. About the
time we finished I hear running on the dock. I go
topside and there is one of the other guys hoofing it up
the dock gesturing wildly, "Fire it up! Fire it up, get
ready to leave!" he's shouting at me.*

"What about the others?" I ask.

*"They'll be here. Just cut everything loose and be ready
to pull off when they get here."*

*So I drop the majority of the lines and start the engines.
We didn't have to wait too long. A couple minutes later
a car screeches to a stop and before it can settle, out
pour the rest of them, high tailing it down the dock.
Even Mr. Luciano is double-timing it.*

*"Cast off! Cast off!" he yells and we do. As soon as
they are aboard, I pull away from the dock. I was just
level with the last pier when I hear three bangs and the
windscreen blossoms three big holes. I duck but keep
going. I hear more gun shots but nothing hits me again
that I know about. And we are through the channel and
out into the open ocean. I can hear a bunch of shouting
and laughing from below, adrenalin wearing off. Mr.*

Luciano comes up top sees the holes and smiles kind of wryly.

"Sorry about that. I didn't expect they would be that unhappy with my payment."

"No problem, but we will need to get that windscreen fixed."

"Yeah, it might draw some attention that way." He laughed briefly.

"Where to?"

"Head for Freeport in the Bahamas. We can take on more fuel there. Then we head to Jersey City."

"That's a long 10 day sail from here. We will need to run through the night and refuel a couple times. I will figure it out."

"Check with me before you put in. I am not as warmly welcomed everywhere."

"Yes, sir."

I wasn't planning on bad weather. The run to Freeport went fine and then on up the coast of Florida and Georgia. That was when we hit the storm. The winds picked up quickly and I heard over the radio the weather report calling for seas of 10-12 feet and winds of 40 knots. This wasn't going to be a fun storm to ride out. All the way up I noticed the boat didn't respond to the steering as well as she usually did and I realized the "banana" boxes in the V-berth were so heavy that the Mist B Haven's bow was digging into the waves more than normal. Not a big deal in regular seas but once the storm hit us it was going to make forward progress very difficult.

I tried explaining that to almost anyone who would listen. Even the guy who had enough experience with boats to have functioned as my relief was unmoved.

"Look, that cargo is a big investment. We are not going to toss it overboard because you don't want to work at steering this bath tub."

I tried to explain how her nose would dig into the taller waves and pull us under causing us to take on more water and be a lot less stable.

"You call me when you get scared and I will come take over."

It was like talking to a kid who thought because he was the best ball player in the neighborhood, he was ready for the big leagues. He had no idea. He wouldn't even start in the bush leagues.

Once the storm started, I asked again if we could consider dumping the cargo to help the boat ride out the storm better. The answer was the same, no. As the waves picked up, the water over the bow became bigger. The bilges are beginning to have trouble keeping up. The bush leaguer who was going to show me how to run the boat is green and is finally starting to get it. Every time water hits the bow the windscreen gets a wash, water pours in the holes and everything including me is wet.

He asked me if I was worried about the windscreen after a particularly big wave. I explained that because it was compromised with the holes, any big water could bust it out and we would be awash with sea water. He puked in the waste basket. I threw it out the door. Mr. Luciano worked his way up top to check on us. The bush leaguer was huddled in a corner moaning. I pleaded with Mr. Luciano one more time to dump the cargo.

"Look, buddy, the only thing that is going over the side of this boat is you and maybe this cry baby here". He gave the puker a kick. "Now buck up and steer this thing. I listened to the weather, too. You got a couple more hours of this and in the meantime start working your way towards shore. Or you wanna swim?"

I said no, I didn't. "Good. Remember they don't call me Lucky for nothing." And he went back out into the weather like he was going to the beach.

Chapter Forty-Nine

I looked back up as a horn began to sound. I realized I hadn't been paying attention. I had been totally absorbed in the story on the pages in front of me. Now I was off course and seemed to have wandered into a shipping lane because off to the starboard side was a big tanker. I adjusted my course and watched as the big ship slid by. I needed to rig up the autopilot. Even if I was at the helm it would help keep me on course if my attention wandered and I could begin to see how much variance there was between what course I chose and where we ended up after a specific period of time.

I kept myself busy for a few minutes setting it up and remembering how to fix the desired course. Once I had it adjusted, I poured a cup of coffee from the thermos I had brought up earlier, scratched Bosco's head enough to wake her up and sat back to watch the water in front of me.

"Ok, Bosco, it seems like the first sheet, from when you tore up the bookshelves, is the first paragraph he wrote, about what was happening on the boat during the storm. These other pages that Charlie gave me this morning are him writing a log entry about what happened. Seems like he hid them in a book and then didn't take them when he jumped off. Maybe he didn't have time to retrieve them. I don't know. But that would explain why that guy at Buddy's wasn't that impressed with the captain. It wasn't the captain he was talking to, but probably this other guy, the bush leaguer the captain called him. They pulled into Pamlico Beach to get repairs done. Then they headed on to Jersey City. I would guess somewhere along there Lucky Luciano transferred off the boat so he didn't alert U.S. Customs and Immigration that he was back in the country. But he left his drugs in the banana boxes to be offloaded and sold in Jersey."

"Holy smokes, Bosco. That means the chances are the money in the hidey-hole in my cabin is the money Lucky Luciano got from that other mobster to set up the family war they were talking about. It is money only he, the other guy and the captain know about. And, according to this, Luciano didn't even want it! How can you not want a couple million dollars? I don't get that!"

She gave me a sleepy-eyed blink.

"Hey, don't go to sleep on me yet! I need to figure this out. I think I need to find out how Stan got this boat and who else owned it. See if anyone else might have put that money there and it isn't the Luciano money. And I still don't know where the other three drawers of bills came from. Boy, I hope Stan gets my letter and can shed some light on this."

"I got a tub full of money and I don't know who any of it belongs to!" Bosco rolled onto her back, stretched and curled back up into a ball. Sleep seemed next on her agenda. She was unimpressed with all the talk. It didn't matter that it was about money. I would do well to imitate her.

I checked the autopilot. It seemed to still be on course and there were no boats in sight, so I went below to fix a sandwich. The rest of the day was pretty much the same. I could see how the monotony of long openwater hauls could make a person a bit crazy. Nothing much changed - water,

water, water. Late in the afternoon I decided to add to the boredom by dropping a fishing line in the water. I went below and pulled out Alf's rod and reel. I had a fake ballyhoo lure so I attached that and paid out some line. Once it was long enough, I set the drag and shoved the rod into the piece of pipe attached to the rail. I went back up top to check to be sure there were no boats on the horizon. Be embarrassing to run into someone because I was fishing!

Chapter Fifty

I sat back down with the book I had been reading, glancing up every page or two to be sure the horizon was still clear. I was just turning a page when I heard the 'zzzzz' of the line paying out from the reel at a fast rate. I jumped up, pulled the boat into neutral, and hopped down to the back deck to grab the rod and release the drag. By the way the rod bent, I knew I had caught something bigger than a gold fish. I started pulling the rod tip up and dropping it as I reeled in as much line as I could. The fish at the other end was strong and didn't want to come to the boat. I kept glancing in front of me to be sure I was still alone on the water. It was harder to land this fish than the ones I had caught with hot dogs. This was a big fish, or it felt like it. I was getting about as tired as the fish when I finally saw it. It came up out of the water trying to escape the hook. Dorado! The yellow and green and aqua colors around its head were sparkling and beautiful. This was some good eating I knew. Alf had offered me some he had frozen when we were in Jersey City. It was very tasty.

I worked the fish close to the starboard stern, caught the line with the gaff hook, and pulled the fish on board. It lay flopping, gills opening and closing trying to breathe. I looked at it laying there, its color starting to fade. I knew I should bang it in the head a couple times with the gaff handle to kill it. But I just couldn't do it. I took the pliers and removed the hook and lure from its mouth, leaned out over the stern gunwale, and held it in the water several feet below me. It lay in my hands floating for a minute, maybe two. The color returned in brilliant shades and it eventually swam out of the cradle of my hands and disappeared.

I rinsed the rod and reel with some fresh water, wiped it down and stowed it away. I would be happier eating beans and rice than eating that beautiful fish. I decided I would stick to hot dog fish, the little ugly inland waterway pan fryers that I had caught on my way down, and leave the deep sea beauties alone.

I went back to the helm, reengaged the engines, reset the autopilot and picked up my book. That had been more than enough excitement for the day. I knew I would have very sore arms tomorrow with nothing to show for it but a good feeling. That seemed like a decent trade.

Chapter Fifty-One

The next couple days were carbon copies of the one before. The autopilot was a great help since it allowed me to read or nap and continue moving towards my destination. I didn't have to concentrate all my attention on driving the boat. I could relax a bit. It made the trip a bit more boring, not so much to do, but I was finding I liked boring. I could do some basic boat maintenance while still being underway. I polished railings and waxed the decks. One day it was calm enough that I could sand and seal some of the mahogany on the upper deck. I was killing a lot of birds with one stone. I had decided to heed Alf and Charlie's warning and was wearing my life jacket all the time. It was getting colder as I got farther north so I usually had a sweater on underneath it. I found the vest helped break the wind and kept me toasty warm as well. I had rigged up a tether as well. I belted it around me, tied a loop and ran the line through and over the rail so I could move around the deck but still be hooked to the boat. It was awkward at first, but like the life vest I had gotten used to it.

I listened to the weather every morning and evening. The storm was still moving slowly and seemed to remain far enough away so as to not really affect me. I was thankful for that, but I still checked on it. I was making good time and expected to make landfall in two days. A total of six coming up the coast. I was more rested than I thought I would be. I had found a rhythm of napping throughout the day so I was awake more at night when it was harder to see what was around me. I liked being awake at night, surrounded by the dark. Plus, I could lay out on the deck and look at more stars than I thought was possible to fill the sky. Away from the bright lights of land, the sky was an amazing thing to behold.

The day before I expected to arrive in Pamlico Beach, I decided to scrub the back deck and gunwales. It was a nice day and the autopilot was set. Bosco was asleep in the salon and I was bored with the book I was reading. Time to do something. I checked the horizon one more time, all clear. Scrubbing could begin. The wind carried the salt up onto the windows and deck, leaving a nice scum on everything if I didn't wash it often. I didn't want to pull into port looking ratty so I washed the windows and mopped the deck. I was wiping down the gunwales on the starboard side when a swell came under the boat shifting me off balance. I grabbed for the rail but missed it and toppled head first into the Atlantic Ocean.

Chapter Fifty-Two

The water was so cold it shocked my system and I couldn't get my breathing under control. I reached for the boat to pull myself back up and realized the boat was moving, but I wasn't. The *Mist B Haven* was motoring away from me! My arms were weighed down by the heavy sweater I was wearing, now soaked with seawater and making it almost impossible to swim. I was still on the surface thanks to the life jacket, but catching up to the departing boat was going to be impossible. Then I felt myself jerked towards the boat. The tether! I was still connected to her! The problem was I was being dragged behind her. I wasn't sure how long the line would hold before the combined weight of me, all my heavy clothes and the strain of pulling me through the water would snap it, leaving me in her wake, floating in the freezing Atlantic. I HAD to get back on that boat!

I couldn't take off my sweater without taking off the life vest and I wasn't going to do that. I pulled the sleeves as close to my shoulders as I could freeing my forearms from the heavy weight and began to pull myself up the line towards the stern of the *Mist B Haven*. I was swallowing a ton of salt water. My head was getting dunked in the wake and I was struggling to breathe. My arms were still sore and weakened from reeling in the fish two days ago. Now I was reeling in an even bigger fish and I couldn't afford to not catch the boat.

It was very slow going as I pulled my body through the water, hand over hand up the tether line. I was silently chanting "Don't snap. Don't snap." As I got closer to the boat I realized I had a second problem. The loop of the tether had followed me along the rail and was now coming off the stern railing just above the still-engaged props. If I approached from the stern I risked either cutting the line on the props or chopping myself up if I got too close and the water sucked me into them. I could also get the line caught in them and foul them. Of the three scenarios, fouling the props certainly seemed like the least horrible but it wasn't good. At best I would foul only one and in the process I would probably be cut loose, still unable to get back on board. I needed a different idea.

I could get myself close to the stern and try to move the tether back up the starboard side away from the props. That would require I not only pull myself to the boat, it also meant I needed to get ahead of the stern to pull the line forward. I was pretty sure that wasn't going to be possible. I decided to just keep dragging myself closer to the boat and hopefully something would occur to me when I got there.

I stopped about five feet out from the stern. I was exhausted and didn't know how much longer I could continue to hold on to the line. My hands had become numb with cold and my arms were almost too heavy to lift. I realized I didn't have any more time to waste thinking of a plan. I tried to position myself dead center of the boat. I would try to come into the stern between the two props, as close to the surface as I could keep myself and hope for the best. I realized I would probably only have the strength for one try. I gathered myself, shoved the sleeves of the heavy sweater up as far as I could, flattened myself out so my feet were on the surface and I pulled myself up to the stern of my boat. I was aiming for the 'B' since that seemed about in the center. I came in as fast as I could and grabbed up at the stern railing. I felt my hand slipping and my feet dropping down into the water closer to the props. I put one arm back in the water long enough to have the current pull my sweater sleeve down over my hand. Then I threw it over the rail, catching the stretched sleeve and holding on tightly. I could hold the wet wool easier than I could the slippery rail. Now I just needed to heave myself and about fifty extra pounds of soaking clothes up and over the gunwale rail on to the deck.

"Easy-peasy," I told myself and, with the last of bit of strength and determination I could muster, I started pulling and kicking my way up and out of the water. I was getting almost nowhere when luck finally showed. A small swell came up from behind me and raised me up towards the boat. I kicked furiously and felt the rail hit my belly. I was almost there! One more big push and I tumbled over the rail onto the deck.

I lay there sobbing and puking and shivering uncontrollably. I knew I wasn't out of danger yet. I needed to get out of these clothes and get warm quickly. My legs were weak and so numb I couldn't feel them. I gave up the thought of walking and just dragged myself across the deck. I made it through the salon and tumbled down the stairs to my cabin and the shower. I lay on the floor of the head almost too exhausted to reach up and turn on the shower. Even cold water felt warm. I pulled myself into a sitting position and began to peel off my clothes adjusting the water as I warmed up. I sat on the floor of the shower until the hot water ran out.

I hauled myself up and dried off, found the warmest clothes I could and put them on. I needed to keep warming myself up. Hot water with honey seemed like the next step.

I could feel my legs a bit now and I willed myself up the stairs and into the galley where I sat while the water boiled. I pulled a jar of honey down off the shelf and dumped half of it in a mug and filled the rest with the hot water. I knew I needed to go check the autopilot and the horizon to be sure we weren't going to hit anything, but I could barely move. A couple swallows of the hot liquid helped, and the honey would kick in pretty soon and give me a little energy. I heaved myself up off the galley bench and slowly climbed up to the wheelhouse. I checked the autopilot, still holding course. Nothing was on the horizon. I pulled the throttles back to slow us down and fell onto the bed behind the helm. Bosco came and settled against my belly and I was asleep before she had curled her tail around herself.

Chapter Fifty-Three

Bosco's crying woke me out of my exhausted sleep. No longer curled against me, she was sitting on the helm ledge looking forward and crying nosily. I rose up gingerly on an elbow. Every part of me hurt. I looked out the window and saw immediately what she saw. A large freighter off my port bow, but close and getting closer. I tried to sit up but my stomach muscles were so sore I couldn't. Instead I rolled out of the bunk and landed hard on the floor. From there, I could pull myself up the wheel and lean against the stool while I disengaged the autopilot as quickly as my swollen, numb hands would allow. I increased the throttles and spun the wheel to starboard. I wanted as much distance as possible between me and the ship before it passed. The water motion around a big ship like this could suck me in closer or swamp me. As I finished turning her to starboard, the horn on the freighter began to sound. Five short blasts, danger. If Bosco hadn't awakened me, that certainly would have, but maybe not in time to avoid a problem.

Alf had warned me that being in the shipping lanes was dangerous, because a lot of the big ships couldn't see over their bows once they got within a quarter mile of a small boat like mine. "They don't mean to run you over. They just can't see you," he had said. I was pulling clear of the wake path and relaxed a bit as the big vessel slid by to port.

"Well, you are certainly one excellent first mate, Bosco! I think you saved our bacon on that one. If only I could teach you to take the boat out of gear when I fall overboard, we would be all set." I sat back on the stool, slowed the engines to a more comfortable speed and pulled the chart closer. I had lost time and position. I hadn't adjusted the autopilot before I collapsed so it held a course that had taken me into the shipping lanes. The reduced speed had set back my arrival time but I didn't care. I needed more sleep and I set a course that would get me out of the shipping lanes quickly so I could rest again.

I checked the horizon and saw only the stern of the ship I had just passed and one other several miles off my bow that I would clearly miss any contact with. I decided some soup and more hot water and honey would be a good idea before I collapsed again.

I was stiff and weak, and my hands were swollen from the salt water and cut and burned from pulling on the rope. While the water and soup warmed I got out the first aid kit and put some salve on my hands and took three aspirin. I sat at the galley table and carefully spooned the warm soup up. My mouth and throat were raw from the enormous amount of salt water I had swallowed and then vomited back up. My stomach wasn't much better since some of the sea water had stayed down and irritated the lining. The soup tasted good and was warm and I knew I needed the energy it would help me build back. Even if it was a bit sore going down, I was happy to be eating it. The honey water helped soothe my throat.

I rinsed the bowl and pan out of habit and set them in the sink to dry. Before I went back to the wheel I rummaged in one of the storage lockers under the seat cushions in the salon to find another life vest. This one wasn't as snug and comfortable as my usual one, but it was better than wearing the still soaking wet one. I vowed I would never be at sea without one on ever. The vest and the tether had saved me. "Thank you, Alf, for suggesting the life jacket and tether. Even when you were mad and disappointed with me, you were still thinking of my well-being. And thank you, Charlie for reminding me it was important to wear the vest even though I thought it was an unnecessary precaution." Bosco looked up from the salon floor where she lay and mewed her agreement. "Yeah, you would have been one hungry cat if I hadn't gotten back on board!" I laughed. But it was true, the boat would have continued on course till she ran out of fuel or ran into something. Either way no one would know what had happened to me. It was a sobering thought. I was beginning to understand just how lucky I had been.

I slowly climbed back to the helm, rechecked my course heading and the autopilot. I wanted to be sure I was clear of the shipping lanes before I lay back down to sleep a bit more. "Okay, you are in charge, Bosco," I murmured as I drifted off.

Chapter Fifty-Four

I slept and woke for the next eighteen hours. My little dip in the ocean had really depleted me. I didn't want to pull into Pamlico Beach and be functioning at half-speed, so I circled out in the open water till I felt physically stronger and mentally sharper. An extra day or two wouldn't hurt anything. It wasn't like anyone was waiting for me. Plus, I hoped the extra time would allow my letter to reach Stan and for him to respond.

I began to feel more like myself in two days but waited one more just to be sure my hands had healed enough to be usable and that I would be able to climb off my boat without groaning and looking three times my age. Any more delay and I knew I would be putting off what I had to do.

Four days after my trip overboard and eleven days after leaving Savannah I pulled into the dock at Pamlico Beach. The same kid was working the dock and accepted my lines with an odd look.

"Yep, I'm back."

He blushed and grimaced.

"Would you mind giving me the phone number you're supposed to call? I can save you the nickel and maybe arrange a more civilized meeting. Or at least one I know is going to happen."

He shrugged and muttered, "If I was you, I would skedaddle right back out into that big ocean and never come here again. But if you want the number, sure, I can get it for you. It's your funeral."

"Well, I hope not, but time will tell. How about we fuel her up and then I'll give them a call."

He ran the hoses to me and while I pumped the diesel into the tanks, he went to the dock shack and came back with a crumpled piece of paper with a number written in smudged pencil on it. "Some guy will answer and you should ask for Frank."

"Okay, thanks."

"Don't thank me. I reckon you're a fool to mess with those guys a second time, but hey, it's a free country."

"Yes, it is." I went up the dock to the pay phone and slipped in a nickel. When a male voice answered, I did what the kid said, I asked for Frank.

"Frank ain't here."

"Well, when do you expect him back?"

The voice laughed in an ugly way in my ear. "No time soon."

I didn't want to deal with this guy. I had no idea who he was. I didn't want to leave a message, not that he was offering to take one. I decided to take a chance and ask for the other name I knew. "Okay, how about Carlo? Is he there?"

"Yeah, but he's busy."

"I think he might want to talk to me. Tell him the *Mist B Haven* is calling."

"Miss who?"

"Bee Haven," I said, figuring it was easier than explaining a boat name to this guy. And if Carlo was the new guy in charge, he would know what it meant. If not, I would probably be holding on to a dead line in a minute or two.

"So, you decided on a return visit," a new voice spoke in my ear.

"Yes, I did. I want to figure out what it is that makes people in Pamlico Beach so interested in my boat."

"I would be happy to come discuss that with you, but I am a little concerned about who else I might meet."

"Huh?"

That brought a chuckle. "Did you return alone, or did you bring a bunch of friends with you to cause me trouble?"

"Ah, no friends, and I really don't want any trouble. I just want to figure out what the deal is and try to straighten things out if that's possible."

"Okay. I don't usually discuss business over the phone."

"Fine. I'm sitting on the dock at the marina. Stop by anytime."

"I might do that. Why don't you have the dock boy, Mikey, call me. I'd like to verify that you are alone."

"Okay. But don't wait too long. I need to keep moving north and the weather doesn't look like it will hold forever." I realized I was talking to nothing. Carlo, if in fact it had been Carlo, had hung up.

Chapter Fifty-Five

At least I had started the ball rolling. I wasn't sure how far it would go or whether when it stopped I would be happy, but at least motion was happening. I went back down the dock to the kid who had finished fueling my boat and was waiting with the bill.

"Do you have a mooring I can rent for a night or so?

"You're staying?" he asked with big eyes and a voice filled with disbelief.

"Yep, I am."

"Well, I know the boss doesn't want any trouble."

"And I am not intending to cause any, though you might say you started the trouble when you made the first phone call and brought those guys to the dock three weeks ago. I am just trying to finish what you seem to have started."

"I didn't mean to start trouble," he grumbled.

"What did you imagine was going to happen when you made that call? That someone would be delivering candy and flowers?" His face took on a glum look.

"I didn't think that far."

"No, you took money from some guys who looked like they were mobbed up and agreed to call them to let them know a certain boat was in port." Now he looked glum and guilty. "I understand that you didn't really think about what that might mean, the consequences of your actions. I have been making similar mistakes myself. But now I need to figure some things out, and as a friend of mine said, I need to grow up. Perhaps you do, too." His head dropped, but he nodded slowly, still looking guilty. "There's a way you can help me if you are willing."

His head came up, but doubt and fear were on his face. "Is your name Mikey?"

"Yeah," he murmured

"Good. I need you to call the number they gave you again and tell Carlo that I'm alone on the boat. Which I am as you can see."

"That's it?" He asked with hope appearing in his eyes. "You just want me to call them?"

"Yep. Just call them and tell the truth. I am here and I am alone. Are you willing to do that?"

"Sure." Relief sounded in his voice.

"And tell them what mooring number I have rented. I assume you will at least rent me a mooring."

"I guess so."

"Good."

"Are there dingys to rent here?"

"Yep. Do you need one?"

"No, but they will. I would prefer that they come out to me. I don't want to be surprised by their arrival this time."

"Okay. Number ten is available and is one of the farthest from the dock so you should have plenty of time to hear them coming."

"That'll work. Thanks. Here's the money for the fuel. How much for the mooring?"

"How about we just call it good?"

"Fine by me as long as it doesn't cause you trouble with the boss."

"Nah, my Dad won't care."

"Okay, then untie me, bow first, and I will go out to the mooring. Then you can go make the phone call."

"Okay. If you're sure that's what you want me to do."

"I'm sure." I went up to the helm and waited while he tossed the lines on board. Then I headed for the farthest mooring ball. I sounded like I was sure, but I wasn't really. I was forming a plan in my mind but I wasn't sure it would work out.

Chapter Fifty-Six

Once I was on the mooring I needed to be sure I could hear any boat approaching. I opened the portholes and the salon door. The problem was Bosco could now wander out onto the deck if she chose. It had seemed that she wasn't that interested so far, but now would be a bad time to have her get interested. I needed everything open, so I closed her in my cabin below decks with her food and water and a litter box and hoped she wouldn't kick up too much of a fuss.

I had told the dock kid, Mikey, I didn't want to be surprised, and I didn't. But I also wasn't sure how soon Carlo would show up, *if* he showed up. It was a wait and see kind of thing. When I was out in the open ocean I had put anything that was liable to wash overboard away. If I couldn't stow them below I lashed them down on deck. I went below to the V-berth where I had stowed two deck chairs I had salvaged in Savannah. I hauled them up and set them out on the back deck. From there I could see anyone approaching from the marina or surrounding bays. I couldn't see the bow, so periodically I would walk up and check the horizon in front of the boat.

The day dragged on. I read and dozed a bit, though I never slipped far from the surface. Deep sleep would have to wait. I put some soup on and fixed a sandwich for lunch. While the soup heated I went below to check on Bosco. Curled innocently on the bed sleeping with barely a head raise when I opened the door. So far so good.

I took the soup and sandwich out on the deck and continued my watch. By late afternoon nothing had stirred from the marina but a couple large sailboats headed out to sea. I decided to start the grill and put on a couple hamburgers for dinner. A nice grilled meal to celebrate not being on the open ocean where beans and rice were the food of the day, every day. The patties browned up perfectly and I tossed a couple buns on the grill to toast. Dinner would be ready for sunset. I set the plate of burgers and potato chips on the small table I had set up next to the deck chairs. And I was just sitting down to the meal when the sound of an outboard motor caught my attention. I looked towards the marina and could see a good-sized dingy heading in my direction. As it got closer I could count three people sitting on the plank seats and a fourth guy crouched in the back by the motor steering the boat.

"Here we go. I hope I figured this right," I said, not sure whether I had actually spoken out loud or just in my head. It didn't matter, they were coming on.

The guy in the back slowed the dingy "Halloo the boat," he called. I realized it was young Mikey from the dock. One of the two guys in the middle of the boat turned and muttered something I couldn't hear clearly at the kid. "What?" the kid said in a fairly loud voice. "She can see us coming. It's not a secret we're here. I would never approach a boat without hailing them."

"Well, ain't you little Miss Manners," the guy said in a threatening voice.

"Hey around here you can get yourself shot at if you don't show some manners."

The guy raised his fist and turned towards the dock boy. "I'll show you some manners, you little..."

"Leave it, Tony," a voice interrupted. "The kid didn't mean anything by it."

"Like hell he didn't," the one called Tony muttered. "Little bastard ought to be taught some respect."

"I said leave it," the guy in the front said in a harsh tone. I knew the voice so it didn't surprise me to see Carlo turn forward and look up at me. "I believe we have some business to discuss."

"Yes, I guess we do," I said. "I would be happy to invite you aboard but I would prefer it was just you. Mikey can stand off a bit with your guys."

"Sounds like a plan. It is just you on board correct?"

"Yep, it is just me and my cat."

"Well, keep it away from me. I'm allergic."

"No problem, she is shut up below. Bring the dingy up to the stern, Mikey. I will hold it off while the gentleman boards." The transfer went smoothly and Mikey backed the smaller boat off from mine.

"I don't like this, boss," Tony called as they floated away.

"We can sit right here on the deck so your men can see you if you like," I offered.

"I'll be sitting right here, Tony. You see anything hinky, you let me know. Otherwise just relax and enjoy the view."

I unfolded the second deck chair and set it across the small table from mine. "I was just getting ready to eat my dinner. Why don't you join me and we can eat and talk."

Carlo sat down in the chair, scooted it a bit closer to the table and smiled. "Burger looks darn good, and I been smelling it practically since we left the marina. You got any mustard?"

Chapter Fifty-Seven

The burgers had proved pretty hard to talk around and I was hungry. So we settled in and ate in silence. When he was finished, Carlo pushed himself away from the table and leaned back. "So I think you have something of value on board this boat that doesn't belong to you."

"Does it belong to you?" I asked, wiping my hands on a wash cloth I used as a napkin.

"I believe it belongs to me more than it belongs to you. How is that?"

"And why is that?"

"Why is what?" He asked puzzled.

"Why do you think it belongs more to you than to me? This is my boat. I bought it fair and square. The title didn't come with a note that said 'This boat belongs to you except for this one valuable thing and even though it is on your boat *that* doesn't belong to you.'"

He stared at me. "Ah, but this is not a "legal" matter. This is not about your boat and who owns what. This is about you have something that is supposed to be mine and I want it back."

"What exactly do you think I have that is supposed to be yours?"

He shifted in his chair as he considered what to say next. "I think you have a large sum of cash on board that is not yours."

"But it is not yours either; it is 'supposed' to be yours."

"It belongs to my family. I am here as their representative."

"How much is a large amount? And how do I know that I won't run into someone else from a different family the next time I stop who says the same thing to me? What do I say to them?"

"They are not sitting here. I am." He shifted again and his suit coat opened to reveal the handle of a pistol tucked under his arm. I'm not sure if he intended for me to see it, but it certainly added a new tone to the conversation. "But if it worries you, you can tell them that they can make a claim on the money by contacting Alfredo Anastasi. My guess is there will be no more questions. Now may I have my family's money? I think Tony has sat in that little boat long enough to make him fairly nervous and seasick. So let's not play cat and mouse any longer. Otherwise I will have to invite him onto your boat and I don't think you would like that."

"I am not trying to be difficult. I just want to be sure I am dealing with the rightful owner. Do you know where this money is supposed to be located?"

"So you did find money on board." That was when I was sure that he didn't really know if there was money still on the *Mist B Haven* or how much was here.

"Some, but I am not sure what you call large amounts."

"Well, we are not talking five dollars."

"Right, I got that. Do you know where it is supposed to located?" I asked again.

"Below in one of the cabins. There is supposed to be a safe of some kind."

"And were you planning on putting this 'large amount of money" in your pocket?"

"He stood and motioned Mikey to bring the dingy in close to my boat. "Hey Tony, bring the duffels and come aboard. You come, too, Geno."

His back was to me as he gestured to his men to come aboard. I reached under the grill and removed the shotgun. I racked a shell and waited. I kept the muzzle pointed low, knee-height, but it would take me but a moment to raise it higher and fire. "I would prefer it was just you, Carlo."

He turned slowly to face me. "Ah, so you took my advice. You got a gun."

"Yes, I did. It seemed like good advice. Now if you would like to continue our business I would appreciate it if you would leave your gun on the deck and ask your men to remove theirs and drop them overboard."

"Are you serious? These things cost money!"

"And you will have plenty, if you do as I ask. If not, well, no money and no legs. Or no wherever I happen to aim." He looked at me, sizing me up as to whether I would do what I said. "I can start by sinking your boat. Hey, fellas, can you swim?" I turned the gun in the direction of the boat and fired a blast near the bow but not quite at it. "Next one doesn't miss." I racked another shell. "Toss the guns overboard now." My voice was loud and as stern as a grade school teacher's. "Carlo, if you want the money all you have to do is keep being a businessman. A small loss for a large gain, I guarantee you."

I could see him considering his options. He knew the money was somewhere below, but not where. I seemed to know exactly where it was. He could do without me, but it would take much longer and success wasn't guaranteed. Plus, he had no way of knowing if I really would use the shotgun on something other than water.

"Do it, boys," he said as he slowly removed his pistol from its holster and set it on the deck. Tony cursed but he and Geno followed Carlo's lead. Two splashes signaled the departure of their guns as well.

"Okay, Mikey. Bring the dingy close and toss the bags on board and then hold off a ways, will you?" The kid was pale but he nodded and maneuvered his bow in to my starboard side and tossed two Army surplus duffel bags up onto the deck. Then he backed away with both men on board glaring up at me. "This should take no more than ten minutes. If I am not back on deck, then head for shore and call the cops. You got that?" Again he nodded.

I motioned Carlo towards the salon, away from the gun lying on the deck. "It will still be here when you come back up. Let's go below and make your family rich."

I motioned him down the stairs with the muzzle of the gun as a pointer. I latched the salon doors and set the shotgun on one of the banquette benches. I didn't want to have the gun with me in close quarters for fear he would take it from me. I didn't think he would hurt me as long as I was showing him the money and I intended to be first back into the salon where I would reclaim the gun. I followed him down below. "It's the cabin with the door closed."

He opened it and stepped in. Bosco was lying exactly where I had left her, curled on my bed sleeping.

"Oh, great. I told you I was allergic, right?" Carlo asked.

"Yes, you did. Sorry, this is the only place I could shut her in. Guess you should work fast."

"So where is the safe?"

"You really don't know?"

"No, but I have done everything you asked, so now it is time to do what I asked. Let's have the money."

"Okay. But I sure hope it is yours and this doesn't come back to haunt me."

"It is ours. Trust me."

I laughed. "Really? You're going with 'trust me'?"

A small smile spread across his face. "Yes, I think I am." He sneezed. "But speed would be good now." He sneezed again. "I won't last long here."

"Sorry." I picked Bosco up and put her out the door.

"Thanks, but that won't help. Just get on with it."

"Okay. The safe is in the floor of the closet. If you stand near the door of the head, I'll open it for you." I picked up the small knife from my desk and went over to the closet, pushed the pile of flip flops and deck shoes aside and began to pry the floor up. I pulled the whole lid off exposing the rows of neatly wrapped bills.

Carlo leaned forward and whistled. "Holy smokes!" he said. "Holy smokes."

"That is exactly what I said when I found it."

He sneezed again. Several times. I could see that his eyes were beginning to redden and swell and his nose was running.

"You best be filling your bags before you go into some major allergic reaction."

"This *is* a major allergic reaction. Jesus! But thanks for your concern."

He squatted by the hole and began to shove packets of money into the first duffel. It filled rapidly and he started on the second. The pile in the hole was quickly vanishing. He was sneezing almost constantly now, but managed to continue to move the money into the duffel.

"Okay. That's it. Get me out of here!' He grabbed a bag and headed for the door. I cut in front of him, opened the door and climbed the stairs two at a time to be sure to get to my shotgun first. It turned out to be unnecessary. Carlo was making a bee line for the salon door and fresh air. I followed him out and looked to be sure that Mikey was still holding the dingy off a ways. He was.

Carlo was doubled over sneezing and gasping for air. "Will you be all right?"

He waved his hand at me in a signal that seemed to say 'yes, give me a minute'. I waved Mikey in closer so the duffel could be transferred once Carlo recovered. It was too heavy and awkward for me to move one-handed and I still wasn't willing to set my shotgun down. Eventually Carlo gained a level of control over his breathing and heaved the bag over the rail, dropping it into the dingy.

"I got one more." He said to his men and turned back into the salon and down the stairs. He returned shortly in more distress but still able to lug the bag over to the rail and drop it as well. He turned to me. "Is there anymore?"

"Are you kidding me?" I replied incredulous.

"Well, it seemed like a good thing to ask."

"Hey, I am running low on fuel. If you want to get back to shore, we should go now." Mikey sounded a bit panicky but still under control. I am not sure how I would have sounded after spending an hour with two pissed off, seasick, wiseguys.

Carlo was still sneezing. His nose was running badly and his eyes were swollen nearly shut.

"Mind if I take my gun with me?" he asked.

"You get in the dingy and I will hand it to Mikey and off you can go. But first I need to know that this is the end of it. There is nothing else on this boat that belongs to you or your family. We are finished here, right?"

"Right. We are finished." Carlo climbed over the rail and Mikey held the dingy steady while he stepped aboard. I leaned down to hand him Carlo's gun. Tony leaped forward and snatched it from my grasp.

"I'll teach you, you fucking little bitch!"

He began to point the gun up at me. I ducked down below the rail as the first shot sailed over my head. I wasn't sure how exposed I was or if Tony would keep shooting. So I reached up and pulled the pin on the grill. The contraption tilted and dumped the still warm coals over the side and into the dingy. I heard one more shot thud into the gunwale just below the railing and just above my head. Tony was finding his range. Then I heard cursing as the coals began to burn the duffels, the dingy and the men. Mikey threw the throttle wide open and raced for shore. I watched as Tony and Geno swatted at the smoldering coals. There was one lone figure semi-standing near the stern of the dingy. I was pretty sure it was Carlo, and I was pretty sure he was waving.

Chapter Fifty-Eight

I sank down into the nearest deck chair and watched the shoreline long after the dingy had disappeared into the marina. I wasn't sure how I was supposed to feel. Mostly I was exhausted. I hadn't slept well or very much at one stretch since I left Savannah. But this wasn't just sleep deprived, though I was. This was a deep exhaustion that followed an adrenaline rush. Entertaining a mobster, even one I found surprisingly amiable had taken its toll. I wasn't in the habit of threatening people with a shotgun or being shot at for that matter! I just sat and stared, unable or unwilling to move.

I wanted to climb into my bed and curl up with Bosco and sleep for days. But I didn't feel safe sitting in Pamlico Beach, even out this far from shore. I didn't want to fall asleep and wake up to find Tony or Geno or whoever standing over me wanting more. I needed to be gone from here. I was just too tired to figure out where to go. I leaned the chair back and shut my eyes. "Just for a few minutes, and then I will get up and get underway."

I awoke in the dark, covered in dew, shivering, with the buzz of a far off motor in my ear. I reached for the shotgun I had propped across my knees. My movement startled something and the motor ceased. "Bosco! How did you get out here?" I looked to see the salon door open just enough to let her slide through. Carlo must have left it unlatched in his haste to get out into the fresh air on his last trip below. I shifted the gun onto the floor and settled the cat in my lap.

"So what brought you out here, may I ask? You aren't supposed to be on deck." She turned her face to me and the motor started up. I scratched her head. "Well, I'm not sure that was a good idea, wandering out here. Though I am glad for your company. I'm not sure giving Carlo millions of dollars was a good idea either. But I am kind of glad it's gone. I guess ol' Lucky Luciano didn't need the money, but Mr. Anastasi will be happy to have it back. At least I hope he is! Now I just have the drawer money to figure out. I guess I need to stay here another day or two in case Stan sent word. I can go check General Delivery tomorrow. But right now I need a hot shower and some sleep." Bosco turned her head towards me, blinked twice and jumped down. "Inside with you, you little rascal." I gave her a gentle nudge with my foot. "No more coming out on deck for you!"

The next time I awoke it was morning, but just barely. The light coming in the port hole was red with sunrise. I got up and went to the galley to start the coffee. The day would be better with coffee. I went back below and closed all the portholes I had opened yesterday. I kicked into a pair of faded jeans, pulled out a clean tee shirt, layered a long sleeved shirt over it and grabbed a sweater. The days were getting cooler and the mornings were definitely cold.

I heard the percolator stop and smelled the coffee as I headed back up top. Coffee in hand I climbed up to the helm to look at my charts for the trip farther north. All I needed to do from here was retrace my steps and run on reciprocal headings back to Jersey City. Bosco hopped up on the chart table and moved to lie down in the center of the chart. "Ah, it's a good thing I need a refill. You can lounge here for a minute or two, but you have to move when I get back." She stretched looking unworried.

When I heard the motor sound from the galley, I was sure it wasn't Bosco purring. This was a motor that sounded like it was getting closer. I pulled on my pea coat, took my fresh cup of coffee out onto the deck and watched as a different dingy approached. It looked like Mikey was running the boat and had one passenger. I set my cup on the flat gunwale and picked up the shotgun. I didn't want to appear unfriendly but I also didn't want to be shot at. I kept the gun low and mostly out of sight until I could determine who was approaching and why.

Mikey throttled back and brought the dingy down off-plane. "Halloo the boat," he called.

"Hey Mikey. What can I do for you?" I didn't recognize the guy hunkered down in his coat until he took off his hat. "Carlo, I thought we were finished." I rested the gun a bit higher so he could see it.

"I thought we were, too, but Mr. Anastasi asked me to return. It's freezing this morning and your coffee looks awfully good. How about you invite me aboard, give me a cup of coffee, and we chat."

"Okay," I said tentatively. "How about you show me you are unarmed?"

"I'm not opening my coat for anyone, I'm too damn cold. I mean you no harm. I promise."

I waited. Not sure I believed him, though I understood not unbuttoning his heavy coat to the wind.

"Trust me." He said with a wry smile. "It worked out okay last time, right?"

"Well, except for the part where Tony tried to shoot me."

"Tony is real sorry he did that," Carlo said as a cold look came into his eyes. "Real sorry."

I waited a moment longer, still unsure whether to send him away or allow him on board. How do I decide that? I thought. But it was easy. He had always treated me respectfully, had defied a superior when he refused to board my boat the first time we met, and had dealt with me in a business-like way. Base your judgments on people's actions towards you and others and then let your gut decide. That's what Alf had shown me.

"Come on in, Mikey. Pull up to the stern. I'll be right back." I went below and filled a thermos with coffee. Grabbed a second cup and went back on deck. The dingy was drawing up on my stern. I looped a line around the front cleat and pulled his bow snug to my stern. "Give this to Mikey and then step across, Carlo." Once he had climbed over the rail I released the dingy. "Just stand off a bit will you, Mikey?"

He nodded. "Thanks for the coffee."

"Hope you like it black."

"Chilly as it is, I would drink motor oil as long as it was warm."

"Well, I hope my coffee is better than motor oil!"

He smiled and backed the small boat away from me. "I'll let you know," he called.

Carlo and I sat down at the table where we had sat last night. He wrapped his hands around the mug and blew on the coffee. "I would invite you inside but I still have a cat and I think you might prefer being cold to an allergic reaction."

"Yeah, here is fine. Thanks for the joe." He said gesturing with the mug. "I am not sure how long it's been since I was up this early. But Mr. Anastasi was very clear that I meet with you before you left."

I sipped my coffee and waited. It seemed like the best idea I could come up with.

"I want to take something out of my pocket and I don't want you shooting me or anything."

"I set the shotgun down when I helped you on board. So okay, I'm not going to shoot you."

He unbuttoned his topcoat and reached into his suit coat breast pocket. He pulled a fat tan envelope out and set it on the table between us. "Mr. Anastasi would like to thank you for your honesty and for returning his property to him. He would also like to pay for any damage Tony's gunfire might have caused you or your boat and appreciates your continued confidence in both these matters. He would also like to extend his friendship to you."

"Friendship?" I sputtered. "Friendship? The guy sent thugs to harass and scare me. No offense meant on the thug part, by the way."

"None taken."

"He paid people to report my movements. He sent guys with guns to take things from me by force, I would guess. I don't really need that kind of friend."

"Ah, you see he thinks you do. That is why he sent me, and just me. Do you have more coffee?" He held out his empty cup.

I snorted, but took his cup and went to refill it, taking mine as well. When I returned he was looking out at the horizon. "It is quite beautiful out here," he said in a wistful voice.

"Yes, it is," I replied, handing him his cup. "And usually very peaceful."

He smiled, blew on his coffee and drank. "It will be peaceful again I promise you. I am only here to deliver this packet and to extend Alfredo Anastasi's friendship. As soon as I finish this," he held up his cup, "I will be gone and you won't see me again."

"It's not that I haven't enjoyed your little visits, Carlo, but I will be happy to really see the end of this."

"Here is what Mr. Anastasi would like his friend to know." He continued as if I hadn't spoken. "The other money you found on this boat is not money. You should not spend it or give it away. You should return to where you came from and give it to the men who meet you at the dock."

"Wha..."

He raised his hand to stop me. "Do not tell the men anything. Just give them the money that they ask you for."

"What do you mean it isn't money?" I asked when it seemed he was finished.

He shrugged. "I can only tell you what Mr. Anastasi asked me to tell you. I don't know more."

"Well thanks a lot for nothing. That makes no sense. The money isn't money."

"I don't know what it means to you. But I do know that Mr. Anastasi thought it was very important for me to find you to give you his message. I also know that Alfredo Anastasi values and protects people he considers his friends. He considers you his friend. If it were up to me, I would do exactly what he said. But of course it is not up to me, it is up to you."

He pushed the envelope towards me. "He is very grateful for the full return of his property and sends this as a token of his appreciation."

I didn't want to touch that envelope, but my hand seemed to have a different idea. It reached across and picked it up. Clearly there was money in it. I could feel the shape of it. I put it back on the table and pushed it back towards Carlo. "I don't want this. I don't want his gratitude or his friendship. I just want to be left alone."

Of course it wasn't true. I did want that envelope. I wanted it very badly, but I wasn't sure I wanted what strings might be attached to it. I didn't want mob money anymore. I just wanted to sail away.

"I understand you think you don't want this money or Mr. Anastasi's friendship. I think you would do well to reconsider. He has offered you a small sum to repair your boat and to express his appreciation for you returning his property to him. Property that in the wrong hands could have meant the end of his family. He is very grateful and would like to offer his friendship for that. Friendship means protection and peace for you. Take this money, take his advice, take his friendship and protection. It will serve you in the long run. Trust me." He smiled a slow smile. "It has served you well so far."

He set down his cup, stood up and motioned to Mikey. "Choices are everywhere," he said as he slipped over the side and into the dingy. "Keep my number. You never know when you might need it." He called over his shoulder.

Mikey handed up the now empty thermos with a nod. "Thanks, it was a life saver." He sat back down and backed the dingy away from the *Mist B Haven*.

For the second time in less than 24 hours I watched Mikey's dingy get smaller as it headed back towards the marina with Carlo standing in the back, waving.

Chapter Fifty-Nine

I washed up Carlo's coffee mug and poured what was left in the pot into the thermos Mikey had returned to me. Then I picked up the envelope Carlo had left and took it, the thermos and my mug up top to the helm station. Bosco was curled in her bed. She lifted her head and gave me a green-eyed stare. "What, you think I should have given it back to him? I thought about it, I really did. But I need money and here is some." She continued to look at me, blinking slowly. "I know, I can hear it too. Money doesn't buy good fortune, or whatever it was that captain wrote. I get that, or at least I am getting it more than I did. But this is money that is being given to me. A thank you gift as it were. I don't know, Bosco. I don't know what to do." The cat blinked. "Maybe I should start by opening it." Though I knew if I opened it, that was one more step towards keeping it, not returning it.

I picked up the envelope, slipped my finger under the flap and tore it open. I pulled out packs of money still wrapped in their paper labeling ribbon. Nestled inside was a sheet of paper. I opened the sheet and looked at the spidery handwriting running across it in a deep blue ink.

Thank you for considering this small token of my gratitude. Carlo tells me he is afraid you will not accept it. I hope you have gotten this far and I can convince you.

You returned to me, in full, property I had invested in a venture that, if discovered, could have gotten myself and many others killed. Because I have recovered it, the safety of my family is secure. Your honesty and willingness to part with such a vast sum is both admirable and rare. I appreciate those qualities and wish to encourage you to continue to exhibit them.

The contents of this envelope are a finder's fee, in a way. A small fraction of the larger amount, but an amount I believe will help you without raising a number of questions. Please accept it, use it to continue on your journey. Sometimes young people need encouragement to make the right choices in life. You did by not keeping what was not yours. It is my hope that this will encourage you to make those kinds of choices again in the future.

Should you ever require assistance of any kind, I would be honored if you would call upon me.

In friendship, and with profound thanks.

Alfredo Anastasi

"What the hell does a mob boss know about making the right choices? Huh?" I asked the now sleeping cat. "A finder's fee. I kinda like that. He is giving me a percentage of something he would have zero of if I hadn't given it to him. I think I can live with that. I did earn it in a way."

Bosco woke up, raised her head and gave me a straight-on look. "Okay, I am trying to convince myself I can keep this money. Is that so wrong?" She gave me the slow sage-like blink. "What would I say to Alf to explain where I got this money? I found millions of dollars under the floor of the closet and when a wiseguy showed up explaining it belonged to his family, I gave it to him. Even though only three other people knew of its existence. When the mob boss got his money back he sent me a thank you gift of", here I paused to count the packs, "fifty thousand dollars. How about them apples? Could I say that to Alf and feel okay about it?" Another sage like blink. "Ah, I think I could. I didn't steal the money, though I could have, and I did think about it. But it is still money that was probably the result of some criminal activity. Does that taint the money? I don't know. But at the moment I am leaning toward keeping it. Maybe I will see how that decision feels over the day and revisit the decision tonight." One more sage blink and Bosco's head drooped onto her crossed legs. She was asleep.

"Fat lot of help you are," I said to the sleeping cat, but maybe she had been. Talking out loud seemed to help me get clearer about what I might do. I would hold off on a decision and wait for a clearer sense of what was the right thing to do.

I finished the last of the coffee from the thermos. It was time to head to shore to check the post office in case Stan had written me.

Chapter Sixty

I nosed the bow of the *Mist B Haven* in to the dock and waited to see if Mikey was around to catch my lines. He stuck his head out of the fuel shack and gave me a wave. "Be right there," he called and disappeared back inside. He reappeared a minute later and tossed a line over the bow cleat and worked his way back to the midship and stern cleats. I turned the engines off and climbed down to the main deck.

I wasn't sure what my reception would be since I had dropped hot coals into his dingy, though he had been happy with the coffee earlier this morning. Still burning holes in someone's boat isn't usually seen as the friendliest thing a person can do.

"Hey, Mikey."

"Hey."

"Sorry about the hot coals in your dingy. Hope I didn't do too much damage."

He laughed. "Well, if you don't mind bailing constantly and blowing in the side tubes about every minute or so I would say I could probably get you a pretty good deal on a used dingy. We almost sank on the way in. The guy who shot at you got a pretty good burn on his hand, but I think Carlo was going to burn him even more once they got out of here. He was pretty steamed that the guy had taken those shots at you."

"Yeah, can't say I was that happy about getting shot at myself." I climbed onto the dock. "I'm headed for the post office. Can I leave the boat here for a bit?"

"Sure, I'll be around. My dad will be pretty mad when he sees the holes in the dingy so I am trying to patch it before he gets here."

"Do you think you can make it seaworthy again?"

"Oh, yeah. They patch up pretty good. It just won't look that good when we go to rent it out. Seeing all the patches can make folks nervous and not trust the boat will get them where they are going. It just makes renting it harder, that's all."

"Well, maybe I should buy it so you wouldn't have to explain it to your Dad. I could use a dingy to get back and forth with. Save fuel bringing the *Mist B Haven* in off a mooring every time I want to go ashore."

"I could give you a good price on it."

"Well, patch away and I'll take a look at it when I get back from my errands."

"Deal."

"Good. See you in a while." I walked up the dock thinking that I could use some of the Anastasi money to fix Mikey's boat. My own boat wouldn't need much repair. A bit of wood putty, some sanding and a little stain where the one bullet hit the railing should make her look good as new. I could pick up the supplies at the marine shop up the street. The dingy would be a bigger project and Mikey was right, no one would want to rent it once they saw all the patches. I could use some of the money to buy the dingy and it would help both Mikey and me.

I turned toward the post office with a lighter feeling than I had had in a long time.

Chapter Sixty-One

General delivery mail is a kind of pot luck. You wait in line and ask if you have any mail and the clerk picks up a batch of letters, sometimes a big batch if it is a popular destination for travelers or a few meager letters if you are off the beaten path or off season. I seemed to be right in the middle. There were enough letters to hope that one was for me, but not so many that the clerk would get impatient sorting through them.

"Nope, got nothing for you." the guy behind the counter said, stuffing the packet of letters back in a cubby hole. "Maybe tomorrow."

"Thanks. I'll check back."

"Mail gets sorted by eleven. Any time after that is good."

I looked at the big clock on the wall that showed it was just after nine. "So you haven't got today's arrivals in that stack yet?"

"Nope. Eleven o'clock."

"Okay, maybe I will stop back after eleven."

"I'll be here." the guy replied.

I went out on to the street. A little breakfast, read the paper and check back seemed like a plan to me. I was pretty sure my boat would be fine on the dock for that long and it would give Mikey more time to work on the dingy.

Buddy's Burgers was the only place in sight and they seemed to be doing a brisk morning business. I went in and sat down at the counter. A cup of coffee appeared in front of me followed by a menu. "Back in a minute," a rather harried waitress said over her shoulder as she moved down the counter with a tray of eggs and bacon. I scanned the menu and settled on two eggs over hard with home fries, sausage patties and toast. I gave the woman my order as she came by headed for the kitchen. The guy next to me finished his breakfast and got up, leaving the paper he'd been reading on the counter.

"Hey, you want your paper?" I asked his back.

"Nah, I only read the sports section and the Bruins didn't play last night. Help yourself."

"Thanks." I settled in with the coffee and the front section hoping to distract myself from wondering if Stan had written. And if he had, what he would say. I hoped it wouldn't be as cryptic as Mr. Anastasi's "the money you have isn't money". Whatever that meant. My breakfast arrived hot and greasy and good. The eggs were firm, not runny, the sausage patties were perfectly spiced and the home fries were crisp and had just the right amount of onion. I really appreciated the food after cooking for myself and I hadn't been eating that well while traveling in the open ocean. This was a treat. I ate everything and sopped up the grease with the last of my toast. The waitress slid my bill onto the counter and swept away my cleaned plate. I was reminded of Lou Anne. I left a good tip along with the money for my meal under the empty coffee cup and took the paper outside. The sun was out and it had warmed up a bit. I sat on the steps of the post office and read the paper until just after eleven.

"Here you go." the clerk separated a thin envelope from the stack and handed it to me.

No return address, but Stan was the only person who knew I was stopping here. It had to be from him. I didn't want to open it standing in the post office. I went back outside to the steps and sat down where I had left the paper. I ripped open the envelope and pulled out one thin sheet of paper.

Not sure what is going on. You should come back. Lou Anne misses you.

I turned the paper over thinking maybe there was more, but there wasn't. Lou Anne misses me? Really? I wasn't sure what to make of Stan's letter. It seemed like all of a sudden everyone was speaking in some other language that I didn't understand. Well, I did understand "come back". And Carlo had said that Mr. Anastasi suggested I also return to where I came from. I guessed that was two votes for heading back up to Jersey City. Might as well throw my vote that way and get going.

I went back into the post office, used one of the chained pens on the counter, and wrote

At the dock sometime Friday. Tell Stan I am coming.

I went back to the clerk and bought a stamped envelope, shoved the paper into it, wrote the coffee shop's address on it and handed it back to the clerk. "Will that go out today?"

"Yep."

"Thanks."

I walked back toward the dock with a stop at the marine supply shop to pick up the wood putty I would need to patch my boat. Mikey was tipped back in a chair outside the fuel shack.

"Hey, you sleeping or thinking?"

"Neither, just soaking in some sun. There won't be any, pretty soon. Winter is coming on." He dropped the chair down on to all four legs and squinted up at me. "Were you serious about buying the dingy?"

I nodded, "Yeah, as long as you don't charge me an arm and a leg."

"Nah, no arms or legs. Does a hundred dollars seem all right?"

"It does if it's ready to go right now. I am getting ready to head out."

"Patches are pretty dry. I wouldn't roll it up yet but if you can leave it out on the deck for a couple more hours it should be good to go. I'll toss in one of our old foot pumps for ten bucks more."

"Sounds like a deal." I pulled some cash from my pants, but then I remembered the other part of Mr. Anastasi's message. Don't spend it or give it away. I shoved it back in my pocket. "Hang on, Mikey, I don't have enough here. Let me get some cash out of the safe. Why don't you get the dingy ready while I go below."

I didn't really have a safe, at least not like a normal person. But I didn't want him to know that. I climbed on board and waited while he went back into the shack to get the inflatable. I raced up top to the wheelhouse and pulled a couple hundreds from one of Mr. Anastasi's packets. I guess I was keeping the money, I laughed to myself.

I was back in the salon when Mikey pulled the dingy out of the shed and laid it on my back deck. He went back and got a duffel bag for the dingy and a second bag as well. "This is the pump," he said, handing me the bag. "Hook it up to the sides first and then once they are pretty well inflated, you can inflate the stern. That will hold the stern board rigid so you can attach the engine. I'm setting you up with a pretty small outboard. It's cheaper and you don't really need a lot of power with this. It will jump up on plane pretty quickly with just you in it. Load it down with a lot of people or stuff and it won't fly, but it will get you home, for sure. I can put the outboard here opposite the grill, tucked in under the gunwale. You can secure it with a couple straps so it doesn't slide across the deck and whack you."

"That would be great, Mikey. Thanks." I wasn't sure the kid had ever said so many words at one time. He seemed almost out of breath.

"Oh, and remember, this is a gas engine, so don't use diesel in it. You got a gas can?"

"Nope, I only use diesel or propane."

"Okay, I think I can find an old one for you."

"Mikey, I think you are either cheating your father or yourself here. A dingy, even a patched one, an engine, a pump and a gas can for a hundred and ten bucks? That doesn't seem right."

He ducked his head and I could see a slight blush hit his hairless cheeks. "I took money from those guys to tell them when you were here."

"I know you did."

"Yeah, well, it wasn't right. I should have minded my own business instead of jumping at the chance for a couple dollars from guys like that. I knew they were up to no good. But I wanted money, so I ignored what I knew. And then they show up and threaten you. I heard them. I saw you with that gaff keeping them off your boat. I was real happy when you left and they were gone. So when you came back, I couldn't believe it. But I swore I wouldn't help them hurt you again."

"And you didn't, Mikey. You warned me when you approached my boat with them on board and you put yourself sideways to the swell for a good long time." His head shot up and he looked at me. "I saw you set yourself up to take as much of the swell as possible. You made those guys seasick. If they had figured out what you were doing, they could have hurt you. But it made them weaker and less able to do anything to hurt me."

"Yeah, but that Tony guy still grabbed the gun and shot at you!"

"Yes, he did. But he missed. He missed partly because he was unsteady on his feet which you had insured by making him seasick, and you were throttling up before he got the second shot off. Both were extremely dangerous actions. So you don't owe me anything. And certainly not a "deal" on a dingy. If anything I owe you. You helped me every chance you got. Thank you."

"I brought them down on you in the first place, so I do owe you."

"Like I said when I pulled in, I guess we both are getting chances to grow up. I, for one, think we both have and are."

He nodded his head. "Yeah, maybe we are."

"How about two hundred for everything?"

"How about one fifty and you don't say anything more?"

I smiled and nodded and handed him two hundred dollar bills. He dug in his pocket and pulled out a crumpled, greasy fifty, flattened it out on his pants leg and handed it to me. He ducked his head and said with a certain level of chagrin, "I charged those guys double to ferry them back and forth."

"Well, I would hope so!" I laughed. "Thanks for everything, Mikey. You are a good kid and you will probably be a good man if you keep making the right choices. I hope you do." I leaned across the gunwale and offered my hand. He took it shyly in his and gave me a firm hand shake.

"You take care of yourself. What I seen the past couple days I reckon you already do."

"You do the same, Mikey. Every time I look at my patched dingy I will think of you and be wishing you well. Now drop my lines before we both start bawling!"

He laughed and moved towards the bow while I went topside to fire up the engines. He waited for my command. "Cast off," I called down from the helm. He dropped the lines and stood watching as I backed the *Mist B Haven* off the dock and headed her out into the sound. I waved and he returned it and then headed back to his chair. I smiled and gave Bosco a pat.

"Okay, girl, we are headed out."

Chapter Sixty-Two

I pulled the charts out and began to figure the fastest, easiest course back to Jersey City. It turned out to be pretty much the reverse of what I had done on my way down, just as I had suspected. I would need to motor a good twelve hours a day to be back on the dock by the time I had picked, Friday.

Days were shorter now than they had been just three weeks ago. The daylight running time was limited. I settled into a routine; get up before sunrise, make coffee, breakfast and fix a sandwich to stash in the fridge for lunch. Be ready at first light to drop the mooring or pull the anchor, whichever I had used overnight. Get underway and have breakfast at the helm while I was running. Around noon I would check my surroundings and if it seemed safe, I would put the boat in neutral, run downstairs to the galley, grab the sandwich and some potato chips and a pop from the fridge and be back at the helm in less than two minutes. Reengage the engines and be underway again. I would run until sunset and use the fading light to drop anchor in a protected cove if I could find one, or pull up on a marina dock and rent a mooring. Then I would cook dinner and check the charts to gauge my progress and make a guess on where I would shelter the next night. I needed to fuel every other day so those nights I rented a mooring for sure. Mr. Anastasi's money was coming in handy, just as he predicted. I turned in early so I would be set to start again early the next morning. This was similar to my usual routine of early to bed, early to rise. It hadn't made me wise, but it was an easy way to function on a boat. There wasn't much night life. A good book was about the only entertainment. That and watching Bosco chase a yarn ball or scrap of paper I would drop for her. This trip, I just made sure to be up and ready to be underway as soon as it was light enough to see what was in front of me.

Days were long and running that much began to take a toll on me. I couldn't really relax or read very much if I was inland on the Intracoastal Waterway. Autopilot is nice but it doesn't work well if other boats are around or in a channel that doesn't run straight. Having to be ever vigilant was tiring. I was looking forward to the end of this trip, even though I wasn't sure what was waiting for me on the dock in Jersey City.

Thursday night I stopped and fueled up so I would have plenty for the trip and in case I needed to leave Jersey City quickly. I opened the floor and pulled all the remaining bills from their hidey-hole. I put them in a brown paper grocery sack from one of my shopping trips and rolled down the top so none could escape. Also in hopes that whoever showed up for it wouldn't count it right away and figure out I had taken over two thousand dollars from the original amount. I wasn't sure what I would do if no one was at the dock when I pulled up. I just hoped Stan had gotten the letter I sent and spread the word of my pending arrival. I took most of the money Mr. Anastasi had given me and put it into the floor "safe" replacing the money now in a bag on the chart table. I didn't want to mix them up and I didn't want anyone to know I had more than what was originally in the drawers.

I shut off the lights, leaving only the white light on top of the wheelhouse that alerted other boats of my position. I warmed up some soup and sat with Bosco on the bench beside me while I ate. "I don't know, cat, I am more nervous about this than I was pulling back on to the dock at Pamlico Beach. I guess at least there I felt like I had a plan. Here, I have no idea what to do or expect. Carlo told me Mr. Anastasi said some men would meet me at the dock and I should give them the money and not say anything. But what if Carlo got the message wrong? What if I am supposed to drop the money somewhere? And how do I know the right 'men' take it from me at the dock? If, in fact, they are there." I paused to eat some of the cooling soup. Bosco curled into a tighter ball against my leg.

"I guess I like it better when I have a plan, even if it doesn't work out. At least I have one. Though I guess I have a plan. Drop the mooring, motor to the marina in Jersey City, pull up on the dock and see what happens. If no one is waiting I will go have a meal at the diner and see what Lou Anne has to say. See, I do have a plan. It just isn't in my control. Not that I had that much control in Pamlico Beach. I just felt like I was thinking it up so I had control. Wasn't really true, but it felt better than this does. Oh, well. Not much I can do but go and see what transpires." I picked up my empty bowl and headed to the sink to rinse it out. Being on a boat, even one as big as mine, had taught me to be as neat as possible, putting things back where they belonged, not letting dishes build up in the sink. It helped keep a sense of order, and clearly I seemed to be a person who appreciated order.

"Come on, Bosco, let's go to bed. I know you will certainly sleep. Maybe that will rub off on me and I will, too."

Chapter Sixty-Three

I was up early. I hadn't slept much and I was getting antsy. It was still too dark to get underway. I was cleaning and polishing, anything to keep busy. I was trying not to make a second pot of coffee but I couldn't imagine running for most of the morning without any more to drink. Tea never seems to be a real option. Who wants to drink tree bark-flavored water? I put another pot on to perk and went below to change clothes. I had been wearing the same tee shirt, jeans and sweater for several days. It is hard to worry about what I am wearing when no one sees me. I pulled out a clean pair of jeans, a long sleeve shirt and a heavy wool sweater. I would grab my pea coat before I went out into the wind. New Jersey in November wasn't really a great place to be a boatie.

The second pot of coffee had finished brewing while I was changing. I filled the thermos and a mug and headed up to the wheelhouse to wait for the skies to lighten enough to get underway. Bosco trailed up after me and settled in her basket on the ledge by the window. The bag of money still sat undisturbed on the chart table. I hoped by this time tomorrow the whole mess would be settled and I would be totally free of other people's money. I had decided if I needed to pay back the two thousand I had used, I would get a job for the winter and stay until I could pay off the "loan". I debated about using some of the Anastasi money but decided to leave that alone and earn what I needed to repay. The fewer questions about where I got my money the better, I figured.

The sun was nearing the horizon; first light was moments away. I hopped down and released the mooring line, eager to get underway.

By the time I could see the cut into the marina in Jersey City it was noon. I had drunk the second pot of coffee and was jumpy and my stomach was sour and doing flip flops, probably from nerves.

"Okay, Bosco, we are heading in. Hope everything works out."

I eased through the cut and approached the dock. I could see Billy shrugging into his heavy coat and pulling on his gloves as he left the warmth of the dock master's shed and came out on the dock to catch my lines. I nosed in slowly, looking up and down the dock as I approached. So far no one but Billy and me.

I slid the door to the wheelhouse open and leaned out into the wind. "Hey, Billy."

"Hey, yourself! Stan said you might be showing up here today."

"Yeah, a little unfinished business, then either I get a job here or I am on down the coast to find one there. "

"Crappy time of year to be here and looking for work, I would say."

"Yep, we'll see. Maybe I will just head for the warm and find a job there."

"That sounds like a better plan," he laughed. "You need fuel?"

"Sure, fill both sides up. Shouldn't take much."

"You want your old slip back? Got your choice right now."
He laughed again, though the wind took most of it.

"The old slip would be fine. Not sure how long my
business will take but I don't plan on leaving again today!"

"Pull her in there once she's fueled. We can figure out
dock fees once you know what you're doing."

"Great."

"Oh, I shut the water down. Seemed like it was going to
freeze the other night. Don't need all these lines freezing up.
Electric is still on though."

"Got it."

"Boy, you were right, she didn't need much fuel."

"Yeah, I fueled last night. Not sure why."

"Always keep her fueled up. Never know when you are
going to want to go somewhere. That was what my old man
used to say."

"Not bad advice."

"You are good to go. I'll drop your lines here and go catch
them at your slip if you like."

"That would be great, Billy, thanks. It's good to see you."

"Good to see you, too, kid. You might want to head up and
see Lou Anne once you get squared away. I know she's
anxious to see you."

"That was my next stop."

Chapter Sixty-Four

Billy headed back to the warmth of the dock house and I slid the door to the wheelhouse closed and looked at the sack of money still sitting on the chart table. I could separate it and stuff it back into the three drawers like I had found it. But then when someone showed up to get it I would have to allow them on the boat or at least make them wait while I retrieved it. I was suddenly much more protective of this money, now that I knew someone was supposed to be coming for it. I didn't want to leave it sitting out in the open while I was gone and I didn't want to carry it around with me. I decided to put it in the upper deck hidey-hole and move Mr. A.'s money (as I had come to think of it) down to the "safe" in my cabin. I figured it had remained undetected with millions of dollars in it for years. Hopefully it would hide my forty-nine thousand and change for a few days.

I checked the dock to be sure no one was headed my way. The coast seemed clear for now. I pulled the floor up and traded the sack of drawer money for Mr. A's money. I shoved the five packets into my waist band and pulled my sweater down over it. No sense in advertising wealth, I thought. I went below to my cabin and repeated the process. Pulled up the closet floor dropped the packets into the extremely large hole and sealed it back up. I replaced my shoes and a few dirty shirts and pants that were stuffed in one corner waiting a laundry run. Everything looked exactly as it had. Satisfied, I grabbed my pea coat and headed up the dock to the coffee shop. Lunch would hopefully quell the roiling in my stomach and soak up some of the caffeine that was still giving me the jumps. And Lou Anne seemed anxious to see me. I wasn't sure what that was about, but I was headed up the dock to find out.

Chapter Sixty-Five

The diner's windows were fogged over so I could barely see inside. It was that time of year; cold outside, warm inside, and foggy windows as a result. I was looking forward to getting warm. If I stayed here very long I was going to have to figure out how to heat at least part of the boat. I didn't want to be shivering all the time.

I pushed through the door and felt the warm, moist air hit my face like I imagine a tropical breeze would. The familiar smell of burgers frying and coffee brewing overwhelmed me. I felt safe here, even if I wasn't. Lou Anne was at the end of the counter. She turned at the sound of the door opening. A big smile spread across her face and she set her coffee pot down to come and hug me.

"Well, lookey what the wind blew in! It is so good to see you, hon!"

I hugged her back and tried to swallow the tears that were threatening to overflow. It just felt good to be somewhere where people knew me. I had been alone or with strangers too long. That was a lesson I would learn over and over until I finally understood that I needed to be alone, but I needed to check in regularly with people who knew me, so I didn't get too far away.

"Sit down. Sit down, hon. You look like you could use some lunch. I have just the thing. Gus made pot roast yesterday and it is really perfect today. I'll get you a plate of that with mashers and gravy, the works. How does that sound?"

"That sounds like heaven, Lou Anne. Thanks."

She pointed me to a booth near the back and disappeared into the kitchen. I sat down huddled in my coat, waiting for the physical warmth of the diner to seep in. The emotional warmth already had. I had stopped worrying about money and men on the dock and what was going to happen next. I was happy just sitting in this familiar place waiting for a plate of food.

When that plate arrived, it was exactly as Lou Anne had advertised. Pieces of beef that fell apart at the touch of a fork, roasted carrots and onions and a big mound of mashed potatoes with thick dark gravy covering it all. "Oh my," I sighed as the smell from the plate wafted up to me. "This is exactly what I need right now."

"Well, good. You eat up and we'll chat once you finish. I want to hear all about your travels!"

"Lou Anne," a voice from the kitchen called. "Give the kid these biscuits, too."

It was all too much for me. I felt the tears overflow and start down my face. I ducked so no one would notice as I dabbed at them with a napkin. I don't think anyone was fooled.

The meal was perfect. Hearty and tasty and very homelike. Comfort food people would begin to call it years later, but then it was just a good hearty meal. This was the first really good meal I had had since the eggs at Pamlico Beach and, like there, I sopped up the last of the gravy with the last of my biscuit. Perfect timing.

Lou Anne slid in across from me just as I popped the last gravy-soaked bite in my mouth. "That was exactly what the doctor would have ordered, Lou Anne. Thanks."

"Got room for cherry pie?" she asked with a bit of a smirk on her face.

"Oh, that was totally unfair! You didn't warn me to save room for pie! I am totally stuffed."

"Well, maybe in a couple minutes after everything settles. Or I can send you a piece to go."

"That sounds like a solution."

"Gus is going to cover me, though it is usually really slow now that the season is pretty much over. So tell me everything! How did it go? How was Alf? How are you?"

"Boy, I hardly know where to start." But not surprisingly, I found a place and for the next half hour I replayed my trip for Lou Anne. I decided to skip the Pamlico Beach part and wait till the end. I wasn't sure how to explain what had happened and I wasn't sure I should. No one but Carlo, Mr. Anastasi and I knew what had transpired. No one else was aware of the second stash of money I had found. As I wound down it became clear to me that no one else *should* know about that transaction. If I told Lou Anne or anyone, it jeopardized Mr. Anastasi. That was what he meant about my continued confidence. That meant my continued silence. I had no real reason to tell that story, at least not right now. Instead I turned it back to Lou Anne and Stan. "So you told Stan I was coming back?"

"I did. I figured something was up when you sent that letter with a post card for me and a letter for him. Then the second one arrived and we knew you were on your way back."

"Yeah. Here I am."

Lou Anne glanced around the diner. There was one guy sipping coffee at the counter down near the register. I hadn't seen him come in. It looked like he hadn't been sitting there long. His cheeks were still red with the cold. She leaned forward across the table and began to speak very quietly. I had to lean forward and strained to hear her.

"Stan asked me to tell you this 'cuz he can't."

"Is he okay?" I asked in a small voice.

"Just listen will you?" she practically hissed. "The guy at the counter is going to follow you to your boat. When you get there get the money you found in the captain's cabin drawers and give it all to him. Don't engage him, just give him the money. If he asks you questions, just shrug and remain silent. Once he is gone, wait half an hour and come back for pie"

"But I spent some, Lou Anne. It isn't all there."

"I know that."

That stopped me for a moment. How could she know I spent some? Though of course she had seen me when I first arrived and I didn't look like a person who could afford to buy a new fridge for my boat or fuel or even eat at the diner very often. Her voice yanked me back to the table.

"How much did you spend?"

"Couple thousand bucks."

"Okay, he doesn't know how much is supposed to be there so I think you should be all right. Just give it to him."

"Okay."

"Pay your bill and go back to your slip. Expect him to show up shortly."

"Okay." I wasn't sure what was going on, but this was almost exactly what Mr. Anastasi's message had said. Give the man on the dock the money and don't say anything. I could do that.

I paid and went back out into the blustery day. I went straight back to the *Mist B Haven* and went immediately to the wheelhouse and pulled up the cover of the hidey-hole. I took the paper sack out, opened it to be sure the money was still in it and replaced the floor. As I was sliding the helm door open I could see a figure approaching on the dock. It looked like the guy from the diner but I wasn't sure. I climbed down the exterior ladder and reached the back deck about the same time as he did. It was the diner guy. I recognized his ruddy face.

"You got something for me?" he asked with a slight snarl.

I handed him the grocery sack. He opened it and looked inside. His eyes widened when he saw what he held.

"You got more of this?" I shook my head.

"You sure?" I nodded.

"Cat got your tongue?" I shrugged.

"Well, maybe I can help you find it." He set the bag on the dock and started towards me with a nasty look on his face. I felt like I had played this scene before. At least I had an idea of what to do this time. I slid over to the grill and pulled the shotgun from its sling. He had gotten one leg over the railing when I racked a round into the chamber. Just like Alf had predicted, it stopped the guy cold. He looked up and I could see his eyes widen as he stared at the barrel of the shotgun pointed directly at him. He slid his weight onto his back foot and began to shift himself back onto the dock.

"Whoa, there, no harm done. Don't shoot that thing."

I waited while he stood up, keeping his hands in a semi-surrender position. He squatted down, never really taking his eyes off the gun, picked up the grocery sack of money he had come for and began to back away. I continued to follow his progress with the barrel pointed at his belly. Once he was far enough away, I lowered the gun from my shoulder but kept it pointed in his general direction until he finally turned and hurried off the dock and out of the marina. I waited to be sure he was gone before I slid down the railing and sat down hard on the deck. I took a couple deep breaths since it seemed like I had not been breathing the last couple minutes. Once my heart stopped racing and I felt like my knees would hold me without wobbling, I got up and replaced the shotgun in its sling. I went into the salon to get out of the wind and cold and to sit down again. Bosco jumped into my lap and began to butt my face with hers, purring in a reassuring manner.

"Well, I gotta tell you, Bosco, Carlo was right. That works way better than the gaff." I wondered how many more times I would have to pull it out to remind some guy of his manners. I sat petting the cat, letting her head-butt me for a few more minutes. Then I went up to the helm station and latched the wheelhouse door. I came back down to the salon and rummaged through one of the under-seat storage bins until I found an old watch cap I had found in the pocket of one of the rain suits left on board. It smelled like old wool but it was dry and would keep me warm. I pulled it over my ears, gave Bosco a final head pat and went out into the late afternoon gloom. It was time for a piece of pie and maybe some explanations.

Chapter Sixty-Six

"You're early." Lou Anne said as I slid on to a stool at the counter.

"Sorry, I lost my watch when I fell overboard and I forgot to wind the clock on the boat. Time seems less important out on the water."

"Mmmm." Lou Anne set a mug of coffee in front of me and turned towards the cooler with the pies, muttering under her breath, something about boaties having their own clock. "Whipped cream or ice cream?" she asked, holding out a big slice of apple pie.

"Ice cream, I guess, though I'm afraid it will make me colder." She nodded and moved to the freezer. "Hey, didn't you promise me cherry?"

"Well, I might have suggested it, but you know the restaurant business. Sell it while you got it. I served the last piece ten minutes ago."

"Darn! If only I had been earlier!" I smiled and so did she.

"Sorry I was a little grumpy. Been on my feet all day and tips aren't good this time of year." She set the plate of pie and ice cream in front of me and topped off my coffee. I knew I probably shouldn't keep drinking coffee, after overdoing it this morning, but it felt warm going down. I needed warm right now.

"So, Lou Anne," I started.

"Eat your pie," she interrupted. "I get off in fifteen minutes and then you and I can go to my place and chat."

"You got heat?" I mumbled around a mouthful of pie.

"Hey, did you lose your manners overboard, too?" she asked in a motherly tone.

"Sorry. Too long eating by myself." I said after being sure to swallow. "Do you have heat at your place is what I asked."

"Of course. It's only fools on boats who don't!"

"You might have a point there. If I stay more than another day or two I am going to have to figure out how to warm up the salon at the very least."

"Space heater. That's what most of the year-rounders do. They get an electric space heater and practically carry it with them around the boat. Gotta be careful you don't start a fire though. It's a fast way to burn your boat to the waterline."

"I can imagine." I pushed my empty plate away and twirled around on the stool. It was dark and the moisture was still high on the window panes. I could barely make out the marina entrance. The *Mist B Haven* was lost in the gloom. I felt exposed on her in a way I hadn't when I was on the dock before. Partly it was because Alf was gone, but also so was just about everyone else. What had once been a crowded marina filled with yachts and sailboats now was just a series of floating walkways and dark water. There was no crowd of boats to obscure the view. It was like a deserted city street late at night when everything was shuttered. I shivered.

Lou Anne's hand on my shoulder interrupted my darkening thoughts. "Okay, hon, let's get out of here." She had put on a heavy car coat and gloves. As we stepped out into the night cold, she threw a scarf around her neck and face. "Winter is coming, that's for sure," she said through the muffle of the heavy yarn. I stuck my hands as deep into the pockets of my pea coat as I could and hunched my shoulders to pull as much of my neck inside the turned-up collar as possible. I followed her around the corner almost running into her when she stopped mid-block.

"Why are we stopping?" I asked, a cloud forming in front of my mouth.

"We are waiting here for the bus." She pointed to the bus stop sign.

"Right." I stamped my feet in an attempt to feel my toes. I silently cursed myself for not buying the socks that guy tried to sell me. I didn't really have shoes or boots for this kind of weather either. "Hope it comes before I turn into an icicle!"

"Oh, for heaven's sake, it isn't that bad!" She laughed and nudged me in the ribs. "Cheer up, it isn't supposed to snow for a couple more weeks!"

"That doesn't help me right now," I grumbled.

The bus pulled up just as Lou Anne appeared to be getting ready to launch into how great winter in New Jersey could be. I followed her onto the bus and dropped in the nickel fare. It was quitting time for most of the dock workers but we had no trouble finding a seat together. We rode in silence. I wasn't sure how far we were going or how I would get back to the marina. Some of the bus lines quit after business hours.

Lou Anne reached up and gave the overhead cord a pull. "This is our stop."

We stepped off and I looked around trying to get my bearings. It looked a lot like the neighborhood I had left months ago. Row houses stretched down both sides of the street. "I'm this way," Lou Anne said, pointing down the left side of the street.

We stopped about half-way up the block and she fumbled in her purse for the key as we climbed the front steps of a three-story row house. The main door opened into a hallway with a staircase directly in front of us. "I have the top unit," she said, beginning to climb. There appeared to be just one unit on each floor, much nicer than the apartment Dominic and I had shared, three to a floor.

Lou Anne unlocked the apartment door, set her purse and gloves on a side table by the door and hung her coat on a hanger in the hallway closet. She took mine and did the same. "Come sit down so we can talk. Shall I get coffee or a beer for you?"

I was cold and tired and my patience was wearing thin. "No, I just want to understand what is happening." I had barely gotten the sentence out when the outer door-buzzer sounded. Lou Anne motioned me into the living room and turned to buzz the door open. She waited by the front door as two sets of heavy feet trudged up the stairs towards us. I wasn't sure if I should look for the fire escape and exit before whoever it was arrived or if I should hold tight and see who it was. My tiredness and the fact that Lou Anne had never been anything but nice to me kept me sitting on her couch. I heard the front door open and Stan and Ned came into the room blowing on their hands and dabbing at runny noses.

"Damn, gals, we were waiting in the car freezing for the past half hour!" Stan grumbled.

"Well, if you would have let me keep the car running we would have been toasty warm! But you are all worried because gas prices just went up a penny."

"Hey, a penny saved is a penny earned." He turned towards me. "Hey, kid, you all right?"

"I should be asking you that, Stan. I am so sorry I left with all that money on board."

He started waving his hand at me. "Whoa, slow down, kid. Let's all sit down and we will try to get all of our stories out and straight, okay?" I nodded. "Good. Lou Anne, I think Ned here needs a hot cup of tea and I guess I could use one, too."

"I'll get a pot going. Why don't you explain to our gal what the deal is, huh?"

Stan sank into an arm chair across from where I sat and looked uncomfortable. He opened and closed his mouth several times but nothing was coming out.

"Okay, girlie, Stan seems to have developed a case of the 'can't talks' so here it is. The money that you found on the *Mist B Haven* was left there for Stan's ex."

"Oh, my god, Stan. I ..."

"Let the man finish the whole story, hon." Lou Anne said from over my shoulder just as the kettle began to whistle.

"Maybe left isn't the best word. Planted would be a better one. It was counterfeit money the Feds wanted Stan to leave on the boat so his ex-wife would find it and take it.

"Hell, she took everything else!" Stan seemed to be finding his voice.

"Apparently she had been laundering money for a small-time hood and was expanding her business beyond Jersey City. The Feds wanted to be able to track the money and her, then lower the boom when the time was right. Stan owed the Feds a small favor, so he agreed to put the money on board. Unfortunately for everybody, she took a vacation and when she got back, you and the *Mist B Haven* were gone and so was the money."

"Billy saw her coming down the dock with a couple guys while I was getting ready to fuel. I was afraid she would try to stop me and take the boat away from me, so I pulled off the dock and just kept going."

"Well," Ned continued after taking a sip of the tea Lou Anne had brought us. "For a while they didn't realize Jorene, Stan's ex, didn't have it. Until banks here in Jersey City started filing reports about bad bills showing up in business deposits. That's when they came after Stan. They figured he had just kept the money and was using it himself. Things got a bit hairy for a while, but I finally convinced them it wasn't Stan spending the money. That refrigerator you bought from Handly's convinced them. Old man Handly remembered you paid in cash and his shop deposit was reported as containing counterfeit bills. So we figured out it was you spending the money. Then a bank outside Atlantic City made a report about a marina deposit and it was obvious you were headed down the Intracoastal spending the government's bad bills along the way."

He paused for another sip.

"Stan, I am so sorry. I should have told you as soon as I found the money. I wasn't thinking of you or anyone else but me. I wanted that money to be mine. It was stupid and selfish."

"You taking off with the money did cause me some trouble, but my smart lawyer there," he pointed over at Ned, "He kept me out of the pokie and once they figured out I hadn't double-crossed them, they settled down a good bit. Then your letter arrived saying you had the dough and would try to get it back to whoever it belonged to. I am not sure what all that stuff about Pamlico Beach was, but I was sure glad to get your note and that you were on your way here. The Feds were pretty happy, too.

"So was it the Feds who came and got the money?"

"No," Lou Anne interjected, "That was one of Jorene's little weasel errand boys.

"But how did she know I was coming back? She didn't even know the money was on the boat in the first place, right? Everyone just assumed if you put it in the drawers, she would eventually find it and take it like she had everything else. Right?"

"That's right. That was my question to the agents, too," Ned said from the kitchen where he was refilling his cup. He came back into the living room and settled back into his chair. "Seems that someone called the hood that Jorene works with and arranged to send some money to be laundered, a trial run to see if they would do more business with them. They told them to meet the *Mist B Haven* on the dock on Friday. The Feds have been tapping his phone, so they heard the call. They didn't know the caller, but I don't think they care. They knew it was you coming back on the *Mist B Haven* and they knew their counterfeit money would end up where they wanted it in the first place, with Jorene.

"So are they going to make trouble for Stan?" I asked.

"Nope. I might even arrange a formal apology for him."

"Nah, totally unnecessary. Just tell them to leave me the hell alone." He smiled and gave me a wink. "Oh, and tell them to leave the kid here alone, too!"

"Well, I don't *tell* them anything, but yes, that will be part of the agreement."

"But what about the money I spent? I need to pay it back or at least make sure all the people who got the counterfeit get real money to replace it."

"The Feds took care of that. They didn't want word to get out that there was counterfeit money floating around. Especially since they supplied it."

"So I owe them?"

"You don't owe anyone, kid." Stan gestured at Ned. "That's what lawyers are for. The Feds just want this to go away. They want you to go away. They are happy that their little sting is still probably going to work. They have no real idea how much is in the bag you passed off to the bagman." He laughed at the words, "So that's how they got their name!" He shook his head. "They want us to forget everything about this."

"Wow."

"That's one way of putting it," Ned chuckled. "I am just glad that we are all here safe and healthy and that Jorene has no idea that Stan was ever involved in setting her up."

"So who did set her up?" Lou Anne asked.

"No idea, but I'm not asking either. That is something I really don't need to know. None of us do."

But I did. I knew. I looked around the room and realized friends were a good thing to have.

Chapter Sixty-Seven

We all sat quietly looking into our tea cups for a moment. I wasn't sure what to say and it seemed no one else did either. I finally took a deep breath and opened my mouth to tell Stan again how sorry I was, but he spoke first.

"I got a feeling you are going to tell me you're sorry again." I nodded. "I understand that and I appreciate you trying to say it again and again. But if we are going to be friends you have to quit. You made a mistake, you wrote me a good letter that explained what you did and why, without making excuses or trying to make it not your fault. You motored back here to make it right. That's what I know and care about. You made a mistake and you owned it and then you did your best to make it right. None of us can do more."

I could feel warm tears trailing down my face. I'm not sure when they started. I didn't know what to say. I used my sweater sleeve to try to brush them away.

"I made some mistakes, too, kiddo. I should have checked that Jorene got the money off the boat. I should never have left you in the position I did. On a boat, with a lot of 'money' and no way to support yourself or that damn boat. I knew you were broke. I could have helped you. But I was selfish, too. I wanted that boat far away from me. I have had nothing but bad luck since I bought it. It reminded me of my missteps and misjudgments, not the least of which was marrying Jorene." A sad smile spread across his face. "So I gave you a broken-down boat and hoped you would sail it right out of my sight. Instead you sailed into a bunch of trouble you didn't even know about. That's the worst part. If I had made sure that the money was gone before I gave you the boat, none of this would have happened.

"I need to apologize for that. I need to figure out a way to make that right. We both made mistakes here, and I reckon we both feel terrible. But that doesn't help us. Feeling terrible doesn't do any good. It just makes us feel terrible and maybe not want to see the other person because they remind us of our screw up. I don't want to be ducking you, kid. I like seeing you. So, what are we going to do so we both can quit feeling lousy?"

"I don't know," I mumbled through the tears. "I think I might always feel bad."

"Well, we can't have that. You are way too young to walk around feeling responsible for this whole thing. Plus, it actually worked out pretty good." He held up his hand and began to count on his fingers. "We all get to see you again. Jorene is probably going to jail. I had nothing to do with sending her there. Ned here got to play with the Feds and ended up getting me a great deal which cost me nothing but Ned's time. And finally I get to try to make it right for you, like you did for me. That's five good things that have come out of this. How about we focus on that, and try to move on as two people who made mistakes and caused someone else harm but who are sorry and mean to be better?"

I nodded, still trying to dry my face. "I would like to try that. But I really am sorry, Stan."

"I know kid. Me too. Now don't say that to me again? Okay?"

"Okay."

Quiet descended again. But this time it felt comfortable and friendly.

"So Lou Anne tells us you fell off your boat!" Ned chuckled. "While it was running! We have to hear *that* story!"

I shot Lou Anne a look. She smiled and shrugged. "It was too good to not tell!" she laughed.

"Okay," I said. "But first I want to know how you all know each other. Because you do, right?"

"Yep, we do. We were kids from the neighborhood," Lou Anne said. "I have known these boys since they were playing stickball in the street. I stayed in the neighborhood; they marched off to war and came back a lawyer and a businessman. But to me they will always be boys in short pants calling me out to play."

I liked that there were people in the world who had known each other for their entire lives. I couldn't imagine it, but I liked it.

"Now come on, give with the taking a swim story," Stan interjected.

So I told them, in great detail and perhaps with a bit of exaggeration for dramatic effect. It was a fish story after all, only I turned out to be the fish. We sat and drank more tea, I didn't mind it as much as I thought I would, and I told them about my travels. Saving Bosco, meeting new people along the way, catching up with Alf in Savannah, the fun of being home and yet in a different place every night. Before any of us knew it, it was late. Stan helped Lou Anne clear away the cups and stayed in the kitchen with her to do the dishes.

"So what are your plans?" Ned asked, leaning forward in his chair.

"I'm not sure Ned. If I really don't owe the Feds or anyone else any money,"

"You don't," he interrupted me to say.

"Well, I still need a job to earn some money to travel on. Fuel and food mostly. I can usually find a place to anchor overnight for free. But right now I am pretty tapped out. Why? You got any ideas?"

"I might," he said leaning back into his chair. "Let me think about it. You will be at the marina, right?"

"Yep, Bosco and I will be huddled under the covers till it warms up a little. That boat is freezing!"

"Yeah, I used to have a sweet little heater," Stan said coming back in from the kitchen. "Till that damn Jorene dragged it off. Probably sitting in my former garage collecting dust! What does she need with an electric space heater?"

"Well, it is on the top of my list once I get a job!"

"Yeah, you have to worry about the water tanks freezing, too. I had them set up with electric heaters. She probably didn't know to take them. How about I stop by tomorrow morning and check on them and if they're still there we can set them up so your pipes don't freeze."

"That would be great, Stan. Thanks."

"Okay, you big lugs, get this young lady home before she falls asleep where she stands." Lou Anne handed me my coat and waited while I put it on to give me a big hug. "You come up and get some breakfast, my treat. Then we'll start thinking about a job for you. In the meantime, go home and don't worry. All will be well."

I hugged her back. "Thanks, Lou Anne. Really, thanks."

"Now shoo all of you!" she said, hugging Stan and Ned before we all set off down the stairs and out into the cold clear night.

Chapter Sixty-Eight

Stan was as good as his word. He was there bright and early the next morning with a good-sized box sitting on the dock next to him. The coffee was just finishing perking, so I grabbed two mugs and went out to greet him with one in each hand. He took his with a smile and stuck his nose in the steam.

"Smells good, kiddo."

"Yeah, I make a mean cup of joe, I've been told. Come on in out of the cold." At least the wind had died and the sun was out today.

"Help me get this on board first." He pointed at the box.

"What is it?"

"Well, it's heavy, for starters! I had Billy drop it off with the dolly."

We wrestled it onto the deck and he motioned for me to open it. I pulled the top open and looked down on a square metal box.

"I think you have to cut the box down the side to open it fully." Stan said as he tried to hand me his pocket knife. I had already figured it out and was opening my own. "Huh, isn't that something. Gal has her own knife."

I blushed a bit. "Well, it just seemed silly to always have to go looking for one every time I need to cut something. Which I discovered, on a boat, is more often that you think. I found this one stuck in a drawer in the wheelhouse. Holy smokes, Stan! No way! You brought a heater?" I finished cutting the box open to reveal a two-foot-cube of a space heater. "Holy Smokes! Thanks"

"The least I could do, since you are back here in the cold thanks to me."

"Hey, we agreed, water under the bridge. No more apologies, or guilt gifts...well, maybe just this one," I grinned.

We shoved it inside and Stan helped me hook it up and start it. "Don't leave it running if you aren't here and don't put anything it front of it. It will get pretty hot. But it's electric so you don't have to worry about killing yourself with carbon monoxide, just with a fire."

I heard a soft thud and Bosco appeared from the galley cupboard, she must have been up in the wheelhouse lying in her bed in the sun. She stopped when she saw Stan. "It's okay, Bosco, this is Stan and he just brought us the best gift ever. A heater!" She crept into the room and sniffed at the warm air around the heater. Then she headed straight to Stan and wound in and out of his legs until he picked her up.

"Hello, little kitty," he said, scratching her under her chin until I could hear her purring across the salon even with the heater pumping away. "Quite the cuddler, huh?" I nodded. Eventually Stan set her down in front of the heater. "This might be the only thing that you let stay in front of the heater." He chuckled. "She'll probably move before she bursts into flame."

I refilled our mugs and we went below to figure out if the water tanks heaters might still be there. We opened the hatch in the companionway. Stan got down on this hands and knees and looked in. "You got a flashlight?"

I went into my cabin and got the big flashlight I kept by my bed. He stuck it in and looked around some more. "Looks like they're there, just not connected. How about you climb down there and I tell you what to do? I don't want to get schmutz on this suit."

"Is that a technical term?" I asked, stepping over him so I could get to the engine room where I stored my tools. "Yeah, it's like schmunda, only different." We both laughed. "Grab pliers, a flat and a Philips head, wire cutters and some connectors if you have them and some electrical tape."

"Aye aye, captain." I opened the engine room hatch and climbed down in to get the required tools. I pulled them from the shelf and shoved them in a cloth bag I kept to carry tools in. It saved me dropping them (usually on my foot) and I didn't have to come all the way back down to get more, since I was willing to carry more than I thought I would need in the bag.

I climbed back up the ladder. Stan was sitting on the floor of the companionway smiling. "Just like the first time we met. I thought you were going to puke on me." He laughed.

"I came close, I gotta tell you." We were both laughing now. "I wasn't sure if I was supposed to go back outside or just throw up in the bilge. I couldn't imagine leaning any closer to that water than I already was."

"Yeah, and then you had to figure out how to get down into the engine room! You got some nice legs on you."

I whacked him hard on the arm. "You weren't supposed to be watching."

"I liked that you decided that you wanted to see everything more than you wanted to be proper." He was rubbing his arm. "You pack a wallop."

"Sorry, I didn't mean to hit you that hard."

"It's okay. I deserved it a little. You look like you are dressed for the job now though."

I looked at the faded jeans and heavy sweater I had put on this morning. The last time I had a dress on was the second day on the boat. Ever since I had been wearing pants. I liked it. "Yeah, I got tired of guys looking at my legs." I laughed again and so did Stan.

I sat down and swung my legs into the now dry bilge, put my hands on either side of the opening and lowered myself down till my feet touched the support struts running the length of the boat. I pulled the bag in with me and took the flashlight from Stan.

"Okay, what am I looking for?"

Stan laid down and stuck his head into the bilge. Fifteen minutes later I had hooked up the heaters to keep the water tanks from freezing and we were back on the main deck sipping coffee in the salon. Bosco was still happily lying in front of the new space-heater and the salon was toasty warm.

"Thanks for this heater, Stan, really. It will be a real life saver. I may never have to wonder where Bosco is again."

"God, I love this boat," Stan said, running his hands along the mahogany paneling and looking around the salon.

"I thought you said it was nothing but bad luck for you."

"I said I have had nothing but bad luck since I bought her. But that doesn't mean I don't love her. She was built by first-rate craftsmen and has great lines. She runs true in the water and turns on a dime. She's comfortable and big enough to have people on board and not trip over them, but small enough to single hand if you want to. Though I guess you know all this."

"I'm learning."

"You've done a really good job of fixing her up, kid. I thought you had it in you but I wasn't sure. Some girls just don't want to get dirty, and not everyone wants to work hard to bring something back to life. She looks happy again. Happier even than when I bought her."

"Where did you get her, Stan?"

"Government auction. She was part of some drug or immigration bust and got confiscated. The government sells that stuff off. It was rumored that at some point Lucky Luciano or some friend of his owned it. But I never knew for sure. Ned did a title search but he couldn't find any hard evidence one way or the other. She was just never lucky for me."

"Well, it might be too soon to tell but at least so far she hasn't been **un**lucky for me. For a while I was thinking of changing her name."

"Oh, don't do that! That will decide it for sure. Very unlucky to mess with a boat's name."

"Yeah, that's what everyone tells me," I shrugged. "I figured I would leave it. And it has kind of grown on me. I think it suits her, and maybe me a little."

"Hmmmm." Stan considered that.

"Not like I'm misbehaving by doing bad things, but more like I am misbehaving by not being what everyone expects me to be. I don't fit into the regular world anymore, Stan. I wear pants and carry a pocket knife, and home is wherever I am. Like that."

Stan was nodding. "Makes sense. I can see it. You are your own person and for a girl that can be seen as misbehaving."

"Exactly!" I smiled. He did get it.

"Well, I don't think it's misbehaving, I gotta tell you. I think it's smart."

"Halloooo the boat."

We looked out the salon windows to see Ned waving from the dock. I jumped up and opened the salon door. "Come aboard and get warm. Stan brought a heater!"

"Boy, it is toasty in here!" I drained the coffee pot and handed him the mug. "So I got some stuff to discuss with both of you," he said as he set his briefcase on the table and motioned us to join him. We all sat down and he began pulling out papers.

"I have been meeting with the Federal Attorney and the State guy as well. I think I have wrung them about as dry as I can. They are worried that one or both of you will sue them."

"Sue them?" I asked "For what? Why?"

"Just let him talk, kid. This is what he does and he is really good at it."

"Okay, but I don't understand."

"Yeah, but you will if you would let him talk," Stan said with a grin on his face. He nodded at Ned to encourage him to start again.

"I didn't say you *could* sue them. I said they are *afraid* you will sue them."

"Oh." I said. Stan rapped on the table and put his forefinger to his lips.

"Sorry." I made the lock-my-mouth-and-throw-away-the-key gesture and he nodded.

"Because they are worried about that, I have negotiated an agreement with them for you both. If you agree to the terms, you can sign these papers and that is the end of it. If you choose not to sign that is fine, but you may end up with the

Feds watching you way more closely than anyone would want to be watched." I must have looked puzzled. "They will wait for you to make some small mistake, not check in with a harbor master when you have been in international waters, make an illegal U-turn, litter, stuff like that. Then they will arrest you and threaten you with major charges unless you agree to sign papers similar to these."

"Okay, wait. Two things, I really need to check in if I have been in international waters?" Both Stan and Ned nodded. "I didn't know that."

"What's two?" Stan asked. "You said there were two things."

"Oh yeah. Well, if they are going to follow and harass me until I sign these papers, why don't I just do it now?"

He pulled a pen from his suit coat pocket and handed it to me.

Chapter Sixty-Nine

"And that, my furry little friend is how we are back in open water heading away from the space heater weather." Bosco was watching me as I set up the autopilot. "Ned negotiated a pay-off for Stan and me. The government would give each of us ten thousand dollars, though they did deduct twenty-five hundred from mine to cover what I 'owed'. Ned wanted to argue it, but it didn't seem worth the trouble. Plus, it was fair. I did spend that money, and they had made good to all the places I had spent it. They also agreed to stop investigating Stan's business. Jorene was his bookkeeper and she had been cooking the books, using his business to hide her little money laundering operation. He seemed real glad to have the Feds close up shop and get out of his hair. He said now he can concentrate on his business again instead of hanging around answering agents' questions."

She began to close her eyes in a sleepy way. "No, no, no, there's more. You can't go to sleep!" She opened her eyes and stared at me as if to say "prove it". "Stan insisted on investing his share of the money for me. He said it was a way for him to feel like he had made it right for me, to make up for some of the trouble he caused me. I tried to tell him I was the one that caused the trouble in the first place by not telling him about the money when I found it. He wouldn't budge. Eventually Ned and Lou Anne convinced me it would make him feel better about the whole mess, so I agreed. The really good thing is now I have an excuse for all the money I have. I can't tell anyone the details of the agreement but I can say I got a government settlement in a legal matter. I am just going to include Mr. A's money in that. And I have an investment account with Stan that will, I hope, grow over time."

Bosco had given up on my story and slipped off to sleep. What did she care about money and the business of the world? She just wanted to be warm and fed. Billy had sold me a small space heater he had used in the dock master's hut for several years before replacing it with a much bigger one. I had lugged it up to the wheelhouse and installed it under the chart table so I wouldn't freeze on my way south. The salon heat didn't make it this far. Bosco was as happy with the arrangement as I was.

I had set the autopilot and was sitting at the helm looking out over the bow at slate gray seas. It would be good to get to warmer, calmer water. Winter was coming and I was glad to be headed away from it. I looked down at the chart. I would be bypassing Pamlico Beach this time in favor of the open ocean route. I thought about Mikey and Carlo and Mr. Anastasi. I had sent Mikey five hundred dollars and a note thanking him for his help and suggesting that he might want to start his own boat for hire business. I wanted to send Mr. Anastasi a note to thank him for his friendship. I knew he had arranged the second Jorene set-up. I wasn't exactly sure how, but I assumed I wasn't his only "friend". He must have known somehow that the Feds were looking for me and the *Mist B Haven,* and why, and he figured out a way to help me. I knew I couldn't write him. I assumed if he knew I was in trouble, he probably knew I wasn't anymore. I would send

Carlo a blank picture postcard once I got farther south. He would know what it meant.

I sat back and thought about friendship and all the people I had met on my journey. Some had meant me harm, but for the most part, people had been kind and generous to me. I turned to look at the large chart of the Atlantic that I had hung on the wall. I had stuck Alf's last note to me on it.

I look forward to meeting you again, to see who you choose to become.

I smiled and leaned forward to check the longitude and latitude of the British Virgin Islands. I might make it by New Year's.

Epilogue

I look back at the seventy-plus year old in the mirror and smile. Lines...but a lot of good times went into putting those on my face. All but Mikey are gone now. He has a big charter service running out of Pamlico Beach. Old age eventually caught up with all but Charlie and Clara. They disappeared in Hurricane Ginger off the coast of Bermuda in 1971 and Carlo died in a mob war in 1980. I miss every one of them. Still.

But I remember. I remember that first New Year's on Jost. Sitting on the upper deck of the *Mist B Haven* toasting the stars with Alf and Charlie and Clara. Telling stories and laughing together about one thing or another. Happy to be with my friends.

I remember.

Acknowledgments

My deepest thanks to all the early readers who encouraged a fragile author and offered gentle suggestions to improve the book: Joann Neuroth, Carolyn Lejuste, Lorie Nachlis, Kathryn Willmore, Barbara Price, Michelle Davis, Daria Hyde, Virginia Hambric, and Kay Cornell.

A huge debt of gratitude to my sister-in-law Susan Steinhagen who cheerfully served as my copy editor, and to Barb Olson, who turned final proofreading into fine editing with sticky notes filled with style suggestions. Any remaining grammatical errors and misspellings are entirely on me!

A big hug to Andrés García-Price for finding the time in a busy life to design and create the cover.

Thanks to my National Novel Writing Month (NaNoWrMo) writing buddy Jamie Archer. Texting my daily word count really helped push me across the finish line.

A wave and a shout out to my former co-workers and guests at Pirates Point Resort, I miss you all. Somehow writing this made me think of you.

ABOUT THE AUTHOR

Photograph of the author by Yvonne Jardine Hubmayr

Originally from Michigan, Martha has had a series of nontraditional jobs since graduating from Michigan State University. She was a printer for nine years, fished commercially, worked for a large outdoor music festival, did research for a law firm, was interim director of a battered women's shelter, drove a delivery truck for a diaper service, an apple orchard and an egg co-op, taught elementary school, painted houses (inside and out), with the occasional bartending and waiting tables thrown in for good measure. She holds a private pilot's license, a commercial truck driver's license, and a U.S. Coast Guard Captain's license.

Martha spent twenty-four years in the Caribbean working as a boat captain and scuba diving instructor before recently retiring to mid-Michigan.

www.ingramcontent.com/pod-product-compliance
Lightning Source LLC
Chambersburg PA
CBHW071103250626
47159CB00002B/584